What They Don't Know

What They Don't Know

A Moonshine Novel

Susan Sands

TULE
PUBLISHING

Prologue

Two Years Ago

"CAN YOU SHUT that stupid dog up?" Jimmy Lee Monroe cast a nasty look toward the anxious pup, which made Bree instantly wary about his aggressive behavior. He had the look of a man who was dealing with a serious mental health disorder—or perhaps some bad drugs. His long hair hung about his face and his eyes flashed with unfocused rage.

"Now, Jimmy Lee, stop being mean to Tiny. He's just a little nervous being that we're someplace new." Jolene Monroe reached out to touch her husband's arm and he pulled back as if she'd burned him.

"Jimmy Lee, can I get you some water?" Bree offered. The couple had come in after calling her office the day before. Luckily she'd had a cancelation and was able to fit them in her schedule. Jolene and Jimmy Lee Monroe had come in seeking marriage counseling presumably, but Bree was seeing red flags concerning Jimmy Lee's behavior. More like flashing neon with accompanying horns blaring.

His eyes refocused on Bree and he nodded, calming a little. "Yeah—uh—sure. Thanks."

Bree kept a water pitcher and glasses on the side table,

mostly for distraction when things got intense, like they were now. She stood and moved away from the couple, giving them a minute to gather themselves. Jolene was whispering to Jimmy Lee as he held his head between his hands. Jolene was thin, with long, honey-blonde hair worn back in a clip. Her dark, heavy mascara had migrated and was smudged beneath her eyes.

When Bree returned with two glasses, she handed them both to Jolene. "So, tell me a little about the two of you so I can get to know you a bit better." The poor puppy who sat in Jolene's lap continued to shiver and whine, darting repeated nervous glances toward Jimmy Lee.

"Well, we met in high school and we've been together ever since. Jimmy's just having a little bit of a struggle with his bipolar disorder right now." Jolene said this almost in a whisper.

Jimmy's tortured gaze fell upon Bree. "It's the meds. They make me crazy."

Ah. "Have you been taking them regularly as prescribed?" Bree asked him.

"I was. But then I ran out of one of them. I didn't have any refills and I couldn't get back to the doctor right away. But I hate how they make me feel, so I'm trying to get off of them."

"Has this happened before?" Bree asked, worried that he'd gone off mood stabilizers or antidepressants cold turkey. If that was the case, he wasn't only chemically unbalanced, he might be in medical jeopardy as well.

Both Jimmy Lee and Jolene nodded.

"Where is your doctor? Are they local?" Bree tried to

keep her voice calm, realizing that if she sounded alarmed, her patients would hear it.

"I don't want to go back there. *Please.*" Jimmy Lee sounded frantic now.

"Do you have family I can call?" Bree asked, hoping Jimmy Lee had a support system.

Jolene and Jimmy Lee immediately locked eyes and shook their heads as if they'd come to an understanding about something. Or someone.

Bree's tone was intentionally calming, her words slow and simple. "Jimmy Lee, you feel this way because your brain chemicals are unbalanced. When you stop taking the medication like that, it's a shock to your system. The only way to feel better is to admit you to the hospital so we can help you get back in balance. If you want this to end, it's truly the only way." Her words were simple and straightforward, and likely they'd both heard them before.

"Just make it stop." Jimmy Lee clutched the sides of his head and moaned.

Bree called 911, which was standard precaution for a patient in the throes of a medical mental crisis. Jolene rather tearfully begged Bree to keep Tiny with her as she rode in the ambulance with Jimmy Lee. Bree agreed because she had very little choice in the matter. And because she'd felt a huge amount of empathy for the scared pup.

The poor guy was shaking and terrified as his momma left him with a complete stranger. "Well, Tiny, I guess we'll have to make the best of this, won't we?" Bree wrapped the little animal in a towel and cuddled him until he finally stopped shivering. She emptied out a small tote bag and lowered the pup into it, and tucked him in with a small, soft towel.

After she'd seen her last patient, Bree headed to the hospital where they'd taken Jimmy Lee Monroe to follow up with his care and return sweet Tiny to Jolene. Bree didn't ask permission to bring him into the hospital, knowing that would require more time than she cared to take. Jolene would have to deal with managing the animal.

Jimmy Lee had been admitted to the inpatient psychiatric ward at North Huntsville Regional Medical Center. She found Jolene in the waiting area. "Any word?"

Jolene shook her head. Bree gently handed the tote bag with a sleeping Tiny inside to Jolene, who thanked her. "The poor little guy wore himself out with worry."

Jolene peeked inside the bag and her expression softened. "My poor baby. He's such a needy little thing."

Bree turned her attention to her patient. "I'll just check in with the nurse's station about Jimmy Lee's condition."

Jolene stopped her with a hand on her arm. "Th-thanks for helping us. We'll be okay now. I'll call his doctor and he'll take over."

"Are you sure?" Bree asked, gleaning from Jolene's expression that she wasn't sure at all.

Jolene nodded and their eyes locked. Jolene suddenly grabbed hold of Bree's wrist and Bree read a soul-deep desperation in her eyes. "Please keep Tiny for me. Just a day or two until I get Jimmy Lee squared away?" She paused. "I know it's a lot to ask from a stranger, but he really seems to like you, and there's nobody else I can trust with him. He's really...*important*."

Bree was at a loss for words. It was a big ask. But her heart broke for the sweet pup who had no place to be while things were turned upside down in his world. "Just for a day or two." Plus, Bree was in the middle of her own personal crisis, and she had to admit that having Tiny to care for was distracting from her own immediate situation.

Chapter One

Now

"DOC, THE PROBLEM is that she's gone and gotten fat, ya know? I mean, you've seen her, right? She doesn't look the same." Ralph Barnes stated this as if Bree Hawthorne, his recently hired therapist, would surely agree with his side of this conundrum. "I don't want to hurt her feelings, but—geez." He visibly cringed.

To her credit, Bree kept her facial expression neutral. "Ralph, didn't Carlee have a baby two months ago?" Critically speaking, Ralph was no prize. He sat firmly on the dad bod side of things as a man in his early thirties, which would've been just fine if he hadn't been in her office specifically to complain about his wife's recent postpartum form.

He nodded, unfazed. "Well, yes she did."

Ralph clearly wasn't an intelligent man, or perhaps he had a brain tumor. Either way, his wasting Bree's valuable time complaining about his overweight wife who'd recently given birth showed a complete lack of good sense. Bree wondered if Carlee had sent him for therapy knowing it might be the only way he would listen to reason, because he'd never take her word for it that he was ridiculous.

Bree took a calming breath, trying to take the most professional route possible despite the urge to smack him upside his foolish head. "Would you say you loved your wife, Ralph?"

"Of course. We've been together since high school. I just hate to see her let herself go like this. My momma got fat and my daddy left her when I was a kid. Never saw him again."

Ah, this was more about his mother than his wife. It often was. "Ralph, people gain weight for all sorts of reasons. One of the most common is growing a baby inside one's body for nine months. I will give you my best clinical advice: don't say a word about Carlee's weight. Ever."

"But—" He started to protest.

Bree held up her hand. "You're paying me for advice right?"

He nodded.

"Carlee's body is full of postpartum hormones right now, which affect her moods, her sleep, and her weight. Her body, emotions, and brain are recovering from producing your precious baby girl." She wanted to say: *If you tell her she's fat right now, she's likely to take a shovel from the barn and kill you with it.* Instead, she said, "Ralph, Carlee is walking a fine emotional line right now. You can do her real harm if you criticize her weight or anything else. It's only been a few weeks since she's created a miracle. Surely you can give her some time to allow her body and hormones to recover."

"Well, I guess that's only fair," Ralph conceded.

"Watch what you say to Carlee. Be helpful and kind. Do what she tells you. She'll lose the weight, and if she doesn't, that's okay too. You promised to love her anyway."

Ralph appeared torn. "I guess things change after babies, huh?"

"They do change, Ralph. And if you want to keep your family together, you'd better change too. And remember that your relationship with Carlee doesn't have anything to do with your parents. You were a child when your dad left and there were undoubtedly many other factors that led to his leaving the family." Bree felt this in her soul from personal experience.

Once Bree had ushered Ralph out of her office, she glanced over to where Tiny, her excessively small Chihuahua mix, lay on the plush pillow napping beside Bree's desk. Tiny opened his eyes upon Ralph's exit as if to say, *yes, Momma, he was an asshole.*

Tiny had become Bree's little soulmate. It was hard to remember life without the precious pup. They'd moved together to Moonshine, Georgia, from just outside of Huntsville, Alabama, almost two years ago after Bree's momma passed, and not long after Bree had broken up with her boyfriend, Doug, a local dentist. Doug had finally bought Bree an engagement ring at Christmas after they'd dated for five years, but two months before the wedding, she'd caught him after hours with his hygienist in one of the operatories, making use of the dental chair in a most unhygienic way. Doug had wasted several years of Bree's biological clock while dragging his feet on making a commitment. It had been a hard lesson.

The job in Moonshine with Moonshine General Hospital had been a godsend in its timing, and it was around that time—just before she'd left Huntsville—that she'd unexpectedly gotten Tiny. So, she'd packed up and taken Tiny with her to start a new life.

Moonshine, Georgia, was a town in the southern Appalachian foothills of the North Georgia Mountains. It was charming, and despite the small population, there were plenty of folks in need of Bree's services. Mental health covered a wide range of issues, and addiction was a major concern in the area.

People sought therapy for lots of reasons. Unhappiness mostly. And there were more reasons for unhappiness than happiness as far as Bree was concerned. She'd like to be proven wrong someday, though. Hope was an elusive bitch, and Bree planned to hang on to it as long as she could, despite patients like Ralph. Hopefully he could gain some enlightenment along the way.

Bree inhaled deeply a couple of times, shaking off the negativity that somebody like Ralph could leave in his wake—in her office.

She gently tucked in Tiny with his favorite blanket into her Louis Vuitton tote. Tiny had gotten used to the bag as his personal space when Bree transitioned here and there. Bree hated to leave Tiny alone for more than a few moments since the poor animal hated to be out of earshot from her.

A WOMAN'S BODY had turned up two days ago at the bottom of a gravel pit in Dalton, Georgia, just east of the Alabama state line. Georgia Bureau of Investigation Special Agent

Mitch Calloway just got word that he'd been handed the case that morning.

As he approached the crime scene, Mitch cleared his mind. Putting himself in the victim's mindset was important. How had she come to be there? Had she suffered? Had she fought? Was she helpless at the hands of her killer? He visualized the incident, filling in the blanks with his imagined version of how things might've gone down. It helped him wrap his mind around the case. He immersed himself into the scene.

Every investigator had their process and their quirks. Mostly, Mitch started with what he envisioned and then allowed the evidence to tell the victim's story. And the perpetrator's.

The forensics team was already there setting up a perimeter around the body—or skeleton was a more apt description. The GBI had been called in to provide support to local law enforcement. Local authorities often didn't have the kind of manpower and specialized investigative tools and labs that the GBI had. In the case of bones, a forensic anthropologist was brought in who specialized in skeletal remains.

The gravel pit had been cleared of most of the heaps of rocks that would've normally been there, according to the foreman who'd found the remains. They'd been prepping the area to do some construction when they'd discovered the bones.

It was hot, dry and dusty, and there hadn't been any rain in the area for at least three weeks. No moisture meant it was less likely they would find any footprints in the rock dust. Of course the place had been tracked up by workers before the body was found, so that wasn't helpful either.

"What do have, Dave?" he asked the investigator who was hovering just over the skull of the body with a camera. GBI special agents and crime scene investigators often knew one another after working cases together over and over.

"Female. Probably early thirties. ID we found confirms it. There's a purse just over here. ID says she's from Huntsville. A Jolene Monroe." He pointed to an evidence bag lying among several others marked with numbers. "Already bagged and tagged it."

"Any prints?"

"None that we could see. There were a few items inside. There." He pointed to more labeled bags. "She was rolled in a tarp, so everything was together."

"Any idea about cause of death yet?" Mitch asked.

The forensics guy shook his head. "Not yet. We'll get the body back to the lab and have a closer look. Not much left of her. Nothing obvious to show what killed her."

"Besides being at the bottom of a few metric tons of crushed rock."

"Yeah. Besides that."

Mitch stood and scanned the area. So many workers had come in and out of here with dozers and trucks. It would be impossible to identify a specific set of boot or tire prints after this long. Now, it was time to go to management and start looking at security footage, assuming there was any. Interviewing every worker who'd been on the ground here since Jolene Monroe's forced interment was another important place to start. Murder investigations were rarely simple, especially when bones turned up.

After loading the photos of the items in the dead woman's purse, Mitch looked more closely at them on his laptop in his car.

They'd uncovered a purse with forty-two dollars in cash, an ID registered to a Jolene Monroe, a maxed-out credit card that hadn't been used since her disappearance, bright pink lipstick, a wadded-up Kleenex, and a phone number scribbled on a fast food receipt from a McDonald's in Huntsville, but no cell phone or keys. The body had obviously been there over a year based on the decomposition—mostly skeletal remains with some hair and clothing. Mitch hoped to hear back soon on the cause of death from the forensic anthropologist once the body was moved to the Whitfield County medical examiner's office in Dalton, Georgia.

He pulled up a photo of the victim on his phone and noted her green eyes and bright smile. In the photo she was holding her very tiny dog. Chihuahua maybe? Not quite. A mix most probably. Cute little thing. He wondered what might've happened to it.

Tomorrow, he would do some research on the life of Jolene Monroe. Who she was, who she associated with, her family, and where they were now. Where she'd worked and lived. And he'd call that phone number they'd found in her purse.

After that, he would drive the two hours to Moonshine, Georgia, to meet with the owner of the gravel pit where they'd discovered Jolene Monroe's remains. He would rather play nice and have the owner willingly cooperate so that the GBI could do a deep dive in his records, security tapes, and employees than have to get a court order. But he'd get one if necessary.

Chapter Two

MITCH STEPPED INSIDE the sheriff's office and allowed his eyes to adjust from the brightness. It was a relief to get out of the Georgia heat and humidity, though it was no worse here than where he'd left it in Alabama, as the case had taken him across state lines to meet with law enforcement in Huntsville, where the woman was reported missing originally.

The drive had been a picturesque one. The area was mountainous and mostly thick with pines and hardwoods, as this part of South Appalachia was in summertime. The Blue Ridge Mountains rarely disappointed.

"Hey there. You must be Agent Calloway." A woman with long, curly brown hair sitting behind a desk with a headset on holding a giant pink Stanley mug firmly in her grasp greeted him.

"Hannah?" Mitch recognized her voice from speaking with her earlier.

She nodded and smiled as she took a sip from her cup and pointed to a chair. "Nice of you to dress up for us."

Mitch shrugged. He always dressed professionally while on the job. In his opinion, it showed respect for the profession. But he realized that Hannah was likely poking a little fun at his wearing a suit in the middle of the summer when nobody else did, so he just smiled and said nothing because no response was required. People poked fun at things that made them uncomfortable or at things they didn't quite understand.

"Have a seat, Special Agent. They're on their way back from Jeb's Diner." She obviously referred to fellow GBI Special Agent Randy Slade and Sheriff Chase Blackburn. "The special's meat loaf and a vegetable today, if you're hungry."

Mitch nodded. "Might head over after we meet." His stomach rumbled. He'd driven over from a quick stop at the Whitfield County medical examiner's office in Dalton, Georgia, after speaking to the forensic anthropologist investigators there. A quick protein shake was all he'd had time for this morning. Plus, an ME's lab didn't do much for the appetite.

Most investigators would've called the medical examiner's office, but as noxious as the smells and shocking as some of the scenes were, Mitch preferred to immerse himself in learning as much as possible when building a full picture of the victim's demise. He wasn't always as welcome as he might wish, but over the years, the GBI anthropologists and MEs had gotten used to him showing up unannounced and looking over their shoulders.

Bells on the front door jingled then, and two tall, brawny men came through. Mitch stood to greet them as they approached. He recognized the fellow GBI special agent immediately. The sheriff spoke. "Hey there, Agent Calloway. Thanks for driving over. You know Special Agent Slade?" He nodded toward Randy Slade, who stuck out his hand.

"Yep. It's been a minute. How's it going, man?" Randy greeted Mitch and the two men shook hands. They'd crossed paths here and there on cases over the past decade. The GBI employed around three hundred special agents all around the state of Georgia.

Mitch wasn't as large a man as the other two. He stood almost six feet, but not quite. Fit but not hugely muscled, he had a runner's body, so standing next to those two might've been intimidating, but Mitch wasn't one to care much about how he appeared next to another man. Over the years he'd learned that they all had something to offer. Wishing to be different had stopped somewhere between high school and college.

"Fine, thanks. Trying to get a handle on this case so we can get the family some closure."

The men nodded. "What've you got?" the sheriff asked Mitch.

"Caucasian female. Early thirties. Around five four. Found her body two days ago in a gravel pit outside Dalton. Looks like she's been there a while. Oh, and the owner of the gravel pit lives here in Moonshine—an Ames Bell of Bell Sand and Gravel."

The sheriff nodded. "The Bell family own sand and gravel pits in several locations all over Georgia and supply construction companies in several states in the southern Appalachian and Blue Ridge region. We can reach out to Ames and get some information on the Dalton location. I'm sure he's heard about the body's discovery by now. Randy here is dating his daughter, Merilee." Chase nodded toward Randy.

Small towns being what they were, this wasn't a surprise to Mitch, so he nodded.

"I'll give him a call. He's semi-retired now and has several managers who run things and report back to him weekly." Randy pulled out his phone.

"I'd like to meet with Mr. Bell as soon as you bring him up to speed on why I'm here. You're welcome to join me if you think he'd respond better to questioning with you present."

"Probably would, I'm guessing. Give me a minute." Randy stepped away and made the call from the other end of the office. The office was comprised of one large room broken up by a reception area, and several cubicles of desks with the sheriff's desk sitting in the front corner closest to the street.

After a couple of minutes, Randy returned. "Okay, we're all set. You want me to drive?"

"Sure, since you know the way."

As Bree locked up her office for lunch, she noticed a well-dressed man coming out of the sheriff's office two doors down from hers with Randy Slade, Moonshine's resident GBI special agent, who was also Merilee's new boyfriend. Merilee owned the salon across the way from Bree's office, and the two women were meeting for lunch at the diner.

There was no way to ignore anyone in this town without it seeming blatantly rude, so she stepped away from the front door of her office and waved at Randy and the handsome but serious-looking stranger. "Hey, y'all."

"Oh, hi Bree. This is Special Agent Mitch Calloway from the GBI. Mitch, this is Bree, our town therapist. She helps us out sometimes with profiling." The man's badge flashed from under his suit jacket, attached to his belt.

"Nice to meet you." Bree nodded and smiled, wondering what kind of case had a second GBI special agent in town.

Calloway gave Bree a hard stare as if sizing her up.

Bree was a big-haired blonde from Alabama—somebody one might imagine as a sorority sister on campus at the University of Alabama (Roll Tide). She *had* attended the university there in Tuscaloosa, but she *hadn't* been a member of a sorority. Despite her scholarships, Bree's family hadn't come close to being able to afford the costs of fraternities and such.

"Nice to meet you, Bree." His tone wasn't convincing. It felt…dismissive. She wondered if he ever smiled or if he'd had enough hugs as a child. When one was trained to try and understand people from limited interaction, one tended to jump ahead sometimes.

"Y'all let me know if you need any help." She waved and turned toward the diner where she was meeting Merilee for lunch. Working with law enforcement was always interesting.

As she walked the block and a half toward the diner, she couldn't get the man's serious expression out of her mind. He was handsome with those piercing dark eyes, yes, but his intensity had gotten under her skin. He appeared stiff and inflexible. Very solemn. He wore a suit to work, which was nearly unheard of in Moonshine. Everybody else around here wore their church boots and starched Wranglers to a wedding. Never on a Tuesday around town. She'd like to get him on her couch for an hour and find out what had caused such an awkward rigidity in his manner. Maybe he'd stopped by on his way back from a funeral. That made the most sense to Bree.

"Oh hey there, Bree." Merilee met Bree at her salon. She was a little early and Merilee was still cutting a client's hair, so Bree busied herself looking at the latest retail items that Merilee offered. She welcomed locally made jewelry, crafts, and food items that were packaged to sell. It was Merilee's way of helping her local small business friends.

When Merilee finished sweeping up the hair and had started a load of towels in the back, the two women headed toward the diner. "Heard they had meat loaf today." Merilee owned the most popular salon in town, and they'd become friends during the time since Bree had moved to Moonshine.

Bree smiled at her friend. "I hope they haven't run out yet." The two women entered Jeb's Diner toward the end of the lunch rush, so odds were that they might be getting low on today's special. There were only a few restaurants in town but only one diner that served breakfast, lunch, and dinner. Jeb's wasn't just a restaurant, it was a meeting place for friends to catch up, dish gossip, and connect.

They snagged one of the recently refurbished Naugahyde booths near the back of the restaurant and were quickly greeted by the longtime server who reminded Bree of a character named Flo on an old show her momma used to watch the reruns of when Bree was a small child. "Hi, ladies. What'll y'all have to drink?"

"I'll have a sweet iced tea with an extra lemon wedge, please, Maevis." Bree double-checked her name tag because Maevis's octogenarian identical twin, Myrtis, also worked there, and both got deeply offended when someone mistook one for the other.

"I'll just have an ice water, thanks, Maevis."

"Be right back."

There were menus, but neither woman bothered, each knowing they were planning to order the meat loaf special. "So, I saw Randy leaving the office a few minutes ago." Bree didn't say any more than that because she didn't want to mention the other GBI special agent, in case they were keeping a new case quiet for now. Merilee would find out soon enough if there was something she needed to know.

"Yes, he texted me that he was going out to speak to Daddy about something."

Bree raised her brows but said nothing.

Maevis returned and took their orders. Thankfully, the meat loaf was still plentiful this afternoon. "So, how are things going at the salon?" Bree asked.

Merilee shrugged. "Busy. Lots of tourists stopping in to ask about last-minute appointments. I always hate to tell them that I book up weeks ahead, so I keep a cancelation list handy in case I get an unexpected opening."

"Yes, weirdly, I've been getting calls from people visiting the area. Seeking therapy isn't usually something people do when they're on vacation. I guess the world has gotten to be a stressful place." Bree had been surprised the first time it had happened.

"Do they just walk into your office?" Merilee asked.

"No, I keep the door locked when I have a patient. They have to call. My phone number is posted outside the front door and on my website." Of course Bree wanted to help as many people as possible, but she drew the line at interruptions when she was with a patient.

They chatted as they ate, and just as Bree took a sip of her iced tea, she noticed a man sitting at the bar wearing a big cowboy hat and nearly choked. *No. It couldn't be.*

AMES BELL AT nearly seventy was an imposing figure sitting behind his very large desk inside his very large home atop a hill at the end of a very long gravel drive. "How can we help you, special agents?" Another man he'd introduced as Joe Dean, one of the managers of Bell Sand and Gravel, stood beside him.

"Sir, we'll need unfettered access to the crime scene and the surrounding area until we wrap up our investigation."

"Of course. No problem. The area is under construction, which is why the pit was being cleared. Otherwise, I doubt they'd have ever found your body." The man frowned in concern. "I'm just glad things worked out the way they did."

Joe Dean cleared his throat. "Uh, sir, we're scheduled to move in some heavy clearing equipment into the area in two days. Logistically, it's a big job—moving that much equipment—it's going to put us off schedule."

Ames looked to Randy. "Son, how long do you think it'll take the bureau to wrap things up?"

Randy looked toward Mitch in question.

"I'm not sure. Maybe two, three days at the most. Coroner has the body. We're taking witness statements from employees, trying to establish a timeline based on forensics, taking soil samples and photographing the area. Depends on what we find." He noticed the usual eyes glazing over as he got into the specifics of discussing their tasks.

Mitch kept a close eye on the body language of everyone he interviewed and saw nothing concerning about Ames Bell. On the other hand, Joe Dean appeared uncomfortable. Likely it was mostly due to the interruption of his work deadline by the investigation. Mitch understood that murder could be inconvenient, but he wasn't prioritizing convenience over a thorough investigation.

"We'll do our best not to drag things out any longer than necessary, sir." He addressed Ames Bell.

The man nodded. "I appreciate it. Thanks for coming out." They all stood and shook hands, and Joe Dean showed them out.

"I don't foresee any issues with Bell getting in the way of things. Do y'all need any help with this one on your end?" Randy asked Mitch as they drove back toward town.

Mitch shook his head. "Not at the moment. We'll see how it plays out. Got some things to run down." His stomach growled as they pulled up at the station. "Might go over and check out the diner."

Randy nodded. "Meat loaf today."

Chapter Three

A S BREE SAT perfectly still inside Jeb's Diner staring at a man who was a dead ringer for Jimmy Lee Monroe, she could hardly breathe. His long hair had been cut and he was wearing a hat, but she'd swear it was him.

"Bree, honey. What is it? What's wrong?"

Merilee's voice penetrated her stunned brain and she shook her head. "That man with the hat over there. Do you recognize him?" Bree nodded toward where Jimmy Lee sat. Thankfully, he wasn't looking their way.

Merilee turned just enough to get a good look at him. "Nope. I've never seen him before. Why? Do you know him?" she asked.

"He looks familiar. Like a patient from a few years ago." Bree forced herself to relax. "It's not a big deal. Anyway, I never approach patients outside of the office due to privacy."

But Bree knew it was Jimmy Lee. She felt Tiny squirm a little in her purse then, and fear shot through her. *What if he'd come back to get Tiny?* There was no way Bree would hand Tiny over to him after the way he'd behaved toward the dog when she'd seen them together. He'd been downright hateful toward Tiny.

"Bree, you're pale. Are you sure you're all right?"

Bree nodded. "I need to go to the ladies' room. Be right back." She scooted from the booth with Tiny in tow, planning to hang out there until Jimmy Lee was gone.

A few minutes later, Merilee came into the bathroom. "That man's gone, if that's what you're hanging out in here waiting for."

Bree was literally standing in the powder room holding Tiny. "Thanks, Merilee. I'm sorry to bail on you like that. It's long story, but I didn't want him to see me."

"Hey, we all have a past. Anyway, he's gone, so you can come on out and finish your lunch. I've got to get back to work. Got a cut and color at one fifteen." She smiled. "Listen, I know you're the therapist around here, but if you need somebody to talk to, I'm here for you."

"Thanks, Merilee. Lunch is on me today. So sorry about that."

Bree went back to the table and was just finishing her meal as she noticed the suit-wearing special agent walking toward her. She smiled at him because good manners demanded that she did.

Calloway acknowledged her with a nod and kept walking, which irked her. "Nice meeting you," she called toward his back. Maybe he was really hungry—or maybe he was just an asshole.

A few minutes later, while Bree was paying her check, a deep voice interrupted her tip math. "Would you like to join me at me at my table for dessert?"

Bree looked up to see Mitch Calloway standing beside her table. Still, he wasn't smiling and he wasn't exactly making eye contact. Her first instinct was to decline his rather curt invitation due to his initial rude behavior, but she was far too curious about this frowny man.

"Okay. I'll be over in a sec." She answered with the same level of enthusiasm with which the invitation had been issued.

Maevis stopped by Bree's table to pick up the check. "Thank ya, honey. Y'all come back soon."

"Thanks, Maevis. Just gonna head over there to join the special agent for a piece of chocolate pie. He's buying." Bree inclined her head toward the booth where Mitch Calloway sat finishing his lunch. His every move was precise. It looked like he'd lined up his utensils, plate and glass just so on the table, which gave her pause. OCD was no joke.

"I'll be over to take your dessert orders in a minute."

Bree slid from the booth and gently picked up her purse with a sleeping Tiny inside. She made her way over to where the odd man sat. He looked up as she approached, made brief eye contact, and motioned for her to take a seat across from him. As unusual as his behavior seemed, he really was an attractive man. Those cool gray eyes were fringed with some seriously thick, curly lashes. But she'd die before she told him that.

"The chocolate pie here is to die for," Bree said as she sat her purse down and had a quick peek to be sure she hadn't disturbed its inhabitant.

"I'm having the cherry cobbler, but you should have the pie if that's what you like." He looked up from his plate and wiped is mouth on his napkin.

"Thanks. I will."

He cleared his throat. "Listen, Bree. I think we got off on

the wrong foot today. I didn't intend to insult you earlier. I got the impression that you were—irritated with me because of my manners."

Bree frowned, not quite sure how to respond. She was noticing signs of stress from him, and her training and experience rose to the surface, superseding that she'd been miffed by his curt dismissal of her earlier. "I'm not irritated with you, Special Agent Calloway. I was a little curious at your manner. But not everybody is as friendly as I am, so I'm willing to start over since you're buying me pie."

A small smile played on those full lips of his, surprising Bree. "You've got a good sense of humor. It's a nice quality. I don't always make a good first impression, so I apologize if I came across as rude. It's something I try to be intentional about—not being rude."

"So, it doesn't come naturally to you? To be polite?" she asked, still so curious about this man.

He shook his head. "No. It doesn't. It's not that I'm impolite on purpose, I just forget that most people expect platitudes and such. I fall on the extreme analytical end of things and often get lost in facts and information. I'm considered on the autism spectrum."

"Ah. I've worked with a quite a few autistic patients." Bree found his admission fascinating. Obviously, he was an extremely high-functioning autistic person—possibly Asperger's—ASD without intellectual or language impairment. That was her best guess having just met him.

"I'm okay with who I am, but it gets me in trouble from time to time. My social interactions aren't always as smooth as I'd like. I solve a lot of cases, so the GBI doesn't seem to mind." He smiled a real smile then and Bree found herself at a loss for words.

Mild autism often caused difficulty with social interactions, so that made sense. "I'm happy to help you with the case if you need it," she offered. Bree had assisted local law enforcement in solving several cases over the course of her career. Profiling was within her wheelhouse.

"Sorry, I can't share any details."

He was a stickler for the rules. Another indicator of his personality. "Fair enough. So, why did you ask me to have dessert?" Bree asked.

"Because I thought it would be a polite thing to do. And you seem like a nice person. I didn't want to leave town feeling like I'd offended you."

"You haven't, so we're good."

"I'm relieved."

MITCH DROVE AWAY from Moonshine feeling a little less embarrassed over his behavior than when he'd obviously offended the lovely Bree Hawthorne. He had a hard time switching gears between focusing on work and trying to use appropriate social etiquette.

He'd worked hard for years trying to blend with the rest of society. After a childhood filled with awkwardness and cringeworthy interactions with peers, his high school counselor had recommended a therapist who'd determined that he was on the autism spectrum. The more he'd learned about how his brain functioned differently, the more he understood why it was so hard to fit in with the other kids—and adults.

Mitch's mom, a nurse, had always tried to teach him good manners but was at her wits' end at his lack of social skills. She was thrilled to find out that he was teachable, despite learning that he was different from his peers. Mitch knew his mother loved him, so she was supportive. His dad—not so much. Dad was a man's man, and when he'd learned that Mitch had a developmental diagnosis, he'd taken it personally.

His parents were both retired now, and living in different towns, thankfully. Mitch didn't see his father much and spent holidays with his mom in Dalton. She was remarried to a nice man named, Tom.

Despite his father's estrangement, the late diagnosis of Asperger's had enabled Mitch to move forward with his life and help him better understand who he was and how best to embrace his gifts and seek support for his social deficits. Just knowing that he was capable of finding balance had given him such hope. Before that, he'd believed that life would always be like that—that he would continue to be an outcast weirdo forever. Social situations still weren't always easy, like today, but they were much better now that he understood how to more effectively navigate them.

Mitch knew that women found him attractive, so he'd dated some in college and since he'd been with the bureau. But relationships were hard. Women seemed to take it personally when he'd forgotten their birthdays or didn't comment on how nice they looked. It was hard to maintain a relationship, especially a new one where every tiny thing he said—or didn't say—mattered so much. It was also very stressful, so dating ranked pretty low on Mitch's current list of important things in life right now.

Solving cases—that's where he got noticed and rewarded. The other special agents didn't care that he was a little weird or robotic sometimes. They only cared that he got the job done.

But he was thinking about Bree Hawthorne right now as he drove home. He'd admitted to her that he was on the spectrum, something he'd never done with a woman. She seemed different. Maybe it was because she was a therapist and she understood a little more about his situation. He got the feeling she wouldn't get her feelings hurt if he forgot to tell her she looked nice—but he couldn't imagine ever forgetting to tell her that. Because she looked *nice*.

Chapter Four

B REE UNLOCKED THE door of her small, two-bedroom, two-bath cabin that sat on the bank of Lake Blue Ridge. She'd gotten really lucky finding this little waterfront gem when she'd moved to Moonshine. No matter what kind of day she'd had at work, the little A-frame cottage welcomed her home like a warm hug, with its gentle slope down to the dock that sat on a quiet cove. She had very few neighbors out here and she rarely missed sitting on her back deck as the sun set over the water.

But today Bree was troubled and had a strong desire to speak to her sister, Darla. Darla was her only connection with family and home, and sometimes, despite the fact that her upbringing hadn't exactly been the picture-perfect kind, it was what Bree craved. She dialed Darla's number as soon as she was settled with a glass of Pinot Noir in her favorite deck chair out back with her shoes off and her feet up. Darla answered on the second ring. "Hey there, honey. How are you?"

"Hey, sis. I'm good. Just getting back into town. Been in Nashville for work for a few days. What's going on in your neck of Georgia?" Darla asked.

"Oh, not too much." Bree shared a lot with her sister,

but she didn't share anything about her patients. Seeing Jimmy Lee so unexpectedly had stirred up Bree's emotions today. So instead of the full truth, she said, "I'm missing Momma, I guess. Just needed to hear your voice." Their mother had been the very sticky glue that had always bonded them. Well, her and Nana, but Nana had died in her sleep from a massive heart attack Bree's first year in college, leaving Darla to deal with Momma at home her junior year of high school.

"Yeah. I drove by the house on my way home from the airport and got a little sad too."

They were both silent for a few seconds. It was hard to control the rush of sadness and regret when Bree thought about Momma—and Nana—and Daddy too. Theirs had been such a troubled relationship. So much love and sorrow.

"How's my buddy Tiny?" Darla was the first to perk up.

"He's good. Sweet and feisty as ever." Tiny was lying atop his favorite pillow on the outdoor sofa, napping. Tiny had a favorite pillow pretty much everywhere he went.

"Give him a kiss from Auntie Darla."

"I will." Bree hadn't told anybody about how she'd gotten Tiny or that her patient who'd left him on her doorstep had gone missing. Discussing her patients was a violation of privacy, and even referring to them without specifics was a line Bree rarely crossed. Bree longed to freely confess her fears about seeing Jimmy Lee, and her worries that he might want Tiny back.

It was a hard thing to keep such a big and important part of her life away from her sister. Darla had always been her bestie, her closest confidante, and her ride or die. She hated not being able to share everything with her.

"Okay. Well, I'm gonna go ahead and get showered."

"Okay, hon. Talk soon."

Why was Jimmy Lee just now coming to find the dog? Had he tracked Bree down here? It wouldn't have been hard given that she hadn't tried to hide her location or identity.

Suddenly, she felt trapped. Trapped by fear that Jimmy Lee had come to find her or come to find Tiny. Either way, she might need help from an attorney or law enforcement. But would they take Tiny from her? Surely not after two years. Bree would need to do some fast case law research to determine who had legal rights to Tiny.

A WOMAN WITH strange eyes—one blue and one brown—led Darla and her to a small room at the back of the new church where there were toys and dolls. "You girls be good now while I get your momma settled." Momma was waiting outside. She was crying, but Bree couldn't remember why.

"Can I give Momma a hug?" Bree asked.

The woman shook her head. "Momma's a sinner. She has to atone with Jesus. After that, she'll be as good as new. Jesus will heal her, and you'll have her back the way she should be."

That sounded pretty good to Bree. Momma hadn't been very nice to them lately; in fact, Momma got really mad when Bree hid her whiskey bottle last week and she'd slapped Bree. Maybe some time with Jesus wouldn't be a bad thing for Momma.

The woman shut the door and she and Darla sat together on the floor, both clutching a doll and each other. This place—this church was new to their family. Daddy had brought them here to help Momma and help him with his two daughters. The women at the church had been kind to them—talking about Jesus. They spent time at the church after school, doing their homework while Daddy was at work. That evening, when Daddy picked them up, Momma stayed at the church and didn't come home for what seemed like weeks.

When they finally saw her again, Momma was a hollowed-out version of herself and she didn't ask for whiskey anymore, but she wasn't the same. Bree wondered if something really bad had happened to Momma at the church because she acted scared, and the women there were so mean to her.

Bree awoke, tears streaming down her cheeks. She hadn't thought about the Followers of Apostolic Faith in years. She wondered if they still operated as a legitimate Christian church, or if somebody had outed them as the quasi-cult they'd been.

Grabbing a glass of water, Bree looked out her bedroom window across the calm surface of the lake. She wondered where Daddy was. If he was even still alive. She and Darla had discussed it many times, wondering if they should try and find him. So far, neither had felt a strong desire to take that huge emotional step. Even when Momma died. It was just too hard.

When Momma had started drinking again, they'd left the Followers of Apostolic Faith, and Daddy had left the family, handing them and their care over to Nana, Momma's mother. When Darla and Bree were old enough, together they learned how to manage Momma themselves, along with Nana. They'd get her into rehab whenever she'd fall off the wagon, get her out, have a good six months with her and then repeat the process. The longest she ever stayed sober was just shy of two years. Those had been the best two years of their lives.

Chapter Five

BREE ARRIVED AT her office the next morning carrying Tiny in her tote and a cup of coffee in her other hand. A sense of foreboding had crawled up her spine and stayed with her ever since she'd seen Jimmy Lee Monroe yesterday at Jeb's Diner.

Today, Bree was scheduled to see three patients—two established ones and one new couple seeking family counseling for their teen daughter. Then, she'd head over to Moonshine General to run her addiction group outpatient therapy. She always brought Tiny with her. Everyone loved him, and she'd gotten permission from the hospital to have him there as the group's mascot.

She set Tiny down on his pillow and lit a eucalyptus candle to cleanse the air. She tried to avoid flowery scents as so many people were allergic to them. Plus, they made Tiny sneeze. As she rinsed her coffee mug, Bree heard the front door to her office open and close. She frowned, realizing she'd forgotten to relock the door after she'd come inside. Her first patient wasn't due for another thirty minutes.

She walked from the back to see who'd come in. Bree's breath caught in her throat and her heart began to pound in her ears when she saw that it was Jimmy Lee Monroe wearing that same cowboy hat he'd had on at the diner yesterday. He stood just inside the front door looking around.

Squaring her shoulders, Bree asked, "Can I help you?"

"Oh, hey there. It *is* you, Doctor Hawthorne. I've been looking for you." His eyes were clear and appeared to be friendly.

"Uh, hi Jimmy Lee. It's nice to see you again. How are you?" she asked.

"I guess you heard about Jolene, huh?" His shoulders slumped a little when he mentioned his wife.

"I haven't heard anything," Bree said.

He shook his head. "Not long after we came to see you, she up and disappeared, and I haven't seen her since."

"I'm so sorry to hear that, Jimmy Lee, but that was almost two years ago. Has something happened lately?" *Why are you here now?* Bree tried to keep her voice steady and her gaze from darting back to where Tiny was sleeping on his pillow in the back office.

"I'm not sure. I figured I needed to start back from the beginning—from where Jolene went missing and retrace my steps, you know? You were one of the last people we talked to before I lost her."

His terminology was odd. *Lost her.* "I'm not sure that I have anything helpful to offer you, but I'm happy to answer any questions you might have." Bree was still a little nervous, but he didn't appear to want to cause her any physical harm at the moment.

"I know she gave you her dog. She told me that she did, and I'm wondering why you?"

Bree froze. "I don't know why she chose me other than I was kind to him that day you went into the hospital. She left Tiny at my house with a note that asked me to take care of him until she could come back to get him. But that's pretty much all the note said. I didn't actually see her again after the two of you left my office."

"Do you still have the note?" he asked.

Bree nodded. "It's at my house. I have a patient due in a few minutes, so I can't go home to get it. But I can show it to you tomorrow if you want to come back."

He shrugged a shoulder. "Okay. I can come back. Is Tiny here?" he asked.

"Yes. He's sleeping in back. Would you like to see him?"

"I wasn't very nice to him, so he might not want to see me. Maybe I'll see him tomorrow. What time can I stop by?" He sounded sincere, which didn't feel threatening at all. He sounded like a man who missed his wife.

"Come back here in the morning around eight o'clock, okay?"

"Thanks, Bree. I'm not here to cause you any trouble. I've been on my meds—I owe that to Jolene. I put her through hell with my mental health problems. The least I can do is keep my sanity while I search for her."

"That's a testament of your respect for her, Jimmy Lee. I know if she were here, she would really appreciate that."

He smiled then. "I hope so."

"I'll see you tomorrow morning."

As he walked out of her office, Bree wondered briefly where he was staying in town.

IT WAS EARLY, but Mitch hadn't been able to sleep much. He'd gotten up and gone for a run, showered, and headed into his office in Calhoun, about thirty minutes south of Dalton, where Jolene Monroe's body was found. His cubicle was small, with a makeshift investigative board tacked up beside his desk. He worked better with an old-school visual. On it, he placed notes, maps, photos, and anything else that might help with his case. Thankfully, Mitch didn't have a partner, as he preferred to work alone.

He was currently on the phone with the GBI's head lab technician.

"The DNA results won't be back for at least a couple of weeks, Special Agent. Maybe longer," the GBI's lab tech reported to Mitch. "We're swamped over here and aren't allowed to make any exceptions. It's all hands on deck after that building collapse in Atlanta. Plus, it's an election year, so lots of promises being made to get results. Your victim doesn't matter to those people. Plus, she's not from Georgia, so far as we know."

"Thanks for your help." Mitch was annoyed. He could control the number of hours he worked per day but he couldn't control the speed at which the lab processed results or how many cases were lined up before his victim.

So, for now, he would use all the circumstantial evidence before them to try and solve this case. Right now, Mitch had every reason to believe Jolene Monroe was killed, wrapped in a tarp, and dumped in a gravel pit almost two years ago, shortly after she was declared missing from Huntsville,

Alabama.

Mitch had some questions for Jimmy Lee Monroe, Jolene's husband, but he seemed to be in the wind. The last hit they'd had on him was at a hospital in Alabama where he'd been admitted to the psych ward. Mitch put a BOLO out to law enforcement, hoping to get a more recent sighting.

He'd pinned up the phone number they'd found in the purse next to the victim. Might as well track that down while he waited to hear something back about Jimmy Lee Monroe or anything about cause of death from the lab.

The call was answered on the first ring. "Thanks for calling the Peterinary Center. How may we care for you?"

"Oh, hi. This is GBI Special Agent Mitch Calloway. I'm calling regarding a woman named Jolene Monroe."

There was dead silence on the line, then the young woman cleared her throat and said, "Jolene no longer works here."

"We're investigating Jolene's disappearance and wondered when you saw her last?"

"The cops came out after she disappeared and asked us all a bunch of questions. We told them everything we knew."

Since they'd not yet announced that Jolene was deceased, Mitch had to tread carefully. "We're just following up on the case, ma'am. Who was the last person there to speak with her?"

"I was. She stopped by on a day she wasn't scheduled to work and said she wouldn't be able to keep her job. Said Jimmy Lee was having a hard time and she had to be with him to help get him through his latest bout with his bipolar disorder. Everybody here knew how hard it was for her to deal with him when he went off his meds."

"When was that exactly?"

"That would've been in September almost two years ago. I remember because the county fair was in town and we always went together."

"Okay. Do you remember if Jolene had a dog?"

"Well, yeah. Tiny was her pride and joy. She loved that little guy." The girl's voice shook a little. "Nobody knows what happened to him. She didn't have him with her the last time she came by. And she *always* had him with her. He was our little mascot here at the Peterinary Center."

"Did she say where he was?"

"No. I asked after him but I could tell she didn't want to talk about it. It was weird. I-I never saw her again after that."

"Okay. Can you take down my number in case you think of anything else that might be helpful? My name is Mitch Calloway."

"Yeah, sure. I've worried so much about Jolene. Gosh, I wish y'all would find her."

He read his number slowly to her. "Thanks again for your help."

The second he disconnected the call, another one came in. It was a hit on his BOLO for Jimmy Lee Monroe. Apparently he'd been spotted in Moonshine. Now, wasn't that a coincidence.

BREE WAS WAITING inside her office when Jimmy Lee arrived the next morning. She'd stopped at the sheriff's office and explained that the man who was coming to her office was a former patient and that he made her a little nervous. She'd asked that Chase check in with her in thirty minutes. He'd requested the name of the man and she'd gladly given it to him. Over the years, Bree had learned that her safety was important. Plus, Jimmy Lee really wasn't a patient and his coming to her office wasn't a secret.

Jimmy Lee entered, seeming to take up more than his share of space in the small foyer of the office. Bree pasted on a smile and spoke to Jimmy Lee. "Hi there. I've got the note from Jolene right here." Bree had read back over it and still couldn't find any reason not to show it to Jimmy Lee, so she handed the handwritten note to him.

> *Dear Bree,*
>
> *Thank you for taking care of Tiny. I'm in a pickle right now and will come back to get Tiny as soon as I can. Please keep him safe for me. I've left some of his favorite toys, his bed, and his food. He's been neutered and doesn't have any health problems. He's very important, so take good care of him, please.*
>
> *I'm so grateful,*
> *Jolene*

His hands shook as he took it. "She always had the neatest handwriting." He read the note and then stared at it. "Thanks for showing it to me."

"No problem. I'm very sorry that she's missing."

"Thanks." He started to turn toward the door, then suddenly spun back toward Bree. "Which toys did she leave for

Tiny? Was there a box or anything? Can you show me?"

When he asked this, he didn't seem sad all of a sudden. It was as if he'd caught a clue and a switch flipped. His behavior made Bree nervous. This was the Jimmy Lee she'd remembered. And in that moment Bree decided that she wasn't telling him anything about anything. Not about the toys or the box.

"Just a couple of his favorite bones and his food in a Walmart sack." The lie left her lips easily, reminding Bree of when Momma had demanded where she'd hidden the booze. She'd looked Jimmy Lee right in the eye and never blinked.

He frowned at her. "Well, all right. Can I see Tiny?"

Bree wanted to say no. But she didn't want to upset a man who she knew to have some real mental imbalance issues. "Um, sure. He's just back here. I'll get him."

Bree's feet were like lead weights. Having Tiny face Jimmy Lee again worried her. She hated that she'd offered yesterday. She picked up her little pal and carried him toward the front of the office just in time to see Chase Blackburn enter. Jimmy Lee didn't react well.

He began to yell and try to get past Chase toward the exit. Bree instantly returned Tiny to his spot in the other room. Once he was back on his pillow, Bree squared her shoulders and headed toward the mayhem.

"You *bitch*!" Jimmy Lee pointed toward Bree. "You set me up. You've got nothing on me. You can't keep me here."

Chase pulled Jimmy Lee's arms behind him, not to cuff him, but to get him to simmer down. "Relax, Jimmy Lee. The GBI found Jolene and they want to have a word with you."

Jimmy Lee dropped to his knees. "They found her? They found my Jolene?"

"I'll let you speak with Special Agent Calloway when he arrives. Until then, I'd like for you to cool your jets at the office."

"Am I under arrest?" he asked.

Chase shook his head and glanced over at Bree. "Not unless you've broken the law. We just need to ask you a few questions."

"She's dead isn't she?" Jimmy Lee burst into tears. "I told Momma she was dead—or she woulda come back."

Chapter Six

BREE DIDN'T KNOW what to think. *They'd found Jolene?* She followed Chase and Jimmy Lee down the sidewalk to the sheriff's office.

"How long until Special Agent Calloway arrives?" she asked Chase. Not because she had been thinking about him at odd times and wondering if she would see him again.

He glanced at his watch. "Within the hour. He put out a BOLO on Jimmy Lee and I contacted him just as soon as you told me he was going to be at your office this morning."

Bree nodded.

Jimmy Lee shot Bree a nasty look. "So you did rat me out."

Bree stood tall and looked Jimmy Lee in the eye. "I always tell the sheriff when I'm going to be alone with someone who makes me uncomfortable. I haven't seen you in a long time until yesterday, Jimmy Lee. And the last time, you were pretty unpredictable."

Jimmy Lee nodded. "I guess that's fair enough. I was pretty out of my mind then. Woman's got to look out for herself. Some bad people out there." He kind of missed the irony of his words, but Bree wasn't going to point that out, knowing how unstable his behavior could be and that he'd just received the shocking news that they'd found Jolene. Chase hadn't confirmed that she was dead, only that she'd been found.

Until today, Bree had wondered what became of Jolene. No, she hadn't come back to get Tiny, but Bree figured it was because things hadn't gone well with Jimmy Lee and her life might have spiraled in a way that being a pet owner didn't support. Bree had tried to call and text the cell number on the paperwork that Jolene had filled out at Bree's office with no luck.

Usually, when patients walked away, Bree let them. Only, the thing with Tiny had been a complication. Bree couldn't very well have reported the woman missing because she abandoned the dog. But she had wondered more than once what had happened to Jolene.

And admittedly, Bree had wondered if Tiny wasn't better off with her than with Jolene as long as Jimmy Lee was nearby. He'd been so unkind to poor Tiny. Maybe Bree should've tried harder to find out what had happened to Jolene. Maybe she hadn't wanted to. Now, she felt pretty bad about that.

And with the GBI getting involved, Bree might have some explaining to do.

"I need to go back and get Tiny." Bree decided she needed a minute to get it together before answering a bunch of questions.

They were inside the sheriff's office now. "Can I speak to you for a second outside, Bree?" Chase asked.

"Um, sure." Bree followed Chase out the front door. They stood on the sidewalk together and Bree was glad there were very few residents out and about this early. "How can I help you?"

"So, what's going on here, Bree? How do you know Jimmy Lee Monroe and his wife, Jolene?"

Bree took a deep breath. "I met them in Huntsville before I moved to Moonshine. They came to me seeking therapy. But only once. This is such a strange coincidence. I'm sure Special Agent Calloway will have the same set of questions since they've found Jolene. Maybe we should just wait on the questioning and do it together." Bree didn't want to have to repeat her story over and over.

"Yeah. That makes sense. He should be here soon. You go check on Tiny and I'll let you know when he arrives."

When Jimmy Lee had asked about the box and the items Jolene had left for Tiny, and Bree lied about them, it was because there was something else. She couldn't put her finger on what it was specifically, but she needed to look inside that box again. She'd kept it because it still had a couple of things inside that Jolene had brought for Tiny that Bree hadn't given him. She'd put it in the closet and pretty much forgotten about it because Bree had started making frequent trips to the pet store and buying things for her new pup.

Tiny sat on his pillow in her office. His big dark eyes were questioning as she stroked his soft, honey-colored fur. "It's okay, boy. Nobody's gonna take you away. Not even Jolene." Bree had a bad feeling that finding Jolene didn't mean they'd found her in a way that meant she was just fine.

There was something about that box that stuck in the back of Bree's mind now. Before, when Jolene had left it, Bree had been in a bad state. The box for Tiny was the last thing on her mind and she'd paid little mind to it. Losing Momma and breaking up with Doug had been so traumatic that everything else was a minor detail. She hadn't even thought about the box again until today when Jimmy Lee had thrust the memory back into her mind. Yes, there was something else.

She didn't have time to run home right now, and Bree had a patient due in a little while. With everything happening, she'd better reschedule the top half of her day at least. This situation wasn't going to resolve itself without a thorough hashing out with the sheriff and special agent.

She spent the next fifteen minutes rescheduling her morning appointments. People in Moonshine were more flexible about that kind of thing than when she'd been working in a city. People here were just more flexible in general, which is one reason Bree liked living here.

Bree kept an eye out for Mitch Calloway as she sat at her desk and reworked her schedule on her laptop while she waited. She had to admit that she anticipated seeing him again. Their last encounter had left Bree with so many questions. He was such an interesting man—clinically. Not bad to look at either.

When he arrived, she noted through the window that he wore a jacket and tie. Not a suit this time, but still. That was like showing up in a tux around here. He was well groomed and looked as if he'd just had a fresh haircut. She'd have to introduce him to Merilee's practiced scissors and clippers. Nobody did a man's high and tight haircut like Merilee.

Bree freshened her lipstick and fluffed her hair like any Southern girl worth her salt would when she was about to be questioned by handsome law enforcement—couldn't hurt. "C'mon, Tiny. Let's figure out what happened to your momma Jolene."

MITCH ARRIVED IN Moonshine in record time. He'd been somewhat shocked to learn that Jimmy Lee Monroe had been spotted at Bree Hawthorne's office this morning. Not to say he hadn't heard stranger things in his line of work. But it was another real coincidence with this case already.

By the time he pulled into the parking space outside the sheriff's office, he found himself anticipating seeing Bree again. The woman had gotten under his skin in a way that few ever had, especially since he'd only met her the one time.

It was unfortunate that he'd need to question her about her association with Jimmy Lee and Jolene Monroe instead of this being a social call. But he really was looking forward to laying eyes on her again.

Chase was waiting for him as he entered the sheriff's office. "Good to see you, Special Agent. I've got Jimmy Lee Monroe in our interview room. Bree Hawthorne's agreed to meet with us after you've had a chance to question Jimmy Lee."

Mitch nodded. "Thanks, Sheriff."

Chase led the way to the interview room. There was an observation area with a two-way glass that allowed law enforcement to watch witness interviews and interrogations. "Camera on?" Mitch asked.

"Yep. We're ready to go."

Mitch took a quick glance through the two-way to ascertain what state Jimmy Lee Monroe was in before heading inside. The man was repetitively tapping his boot on the floor, showing him to be anxious about their meeting. He squirmed in his seat and his eyes darted to and fro. "Looks like he's worried about something."

"He's thinking his wife is dead." Chase filled Mitch in on what had transpired earlier in Bree's office and handed Mitch a file folder.

Mitch read the few sentences of notes that Chase had jotted down. "Thanks."

Mitch entered the room and pulled out the metal chair across from Jimmy Lee and introduced himself. "I'm Special Agent Mitch Calloway with the Georgia Bureau of Investigation. It's nice to meet you, Jimmy Lee." He hoped to put the anxious man at ease a little.

"Did you find her? Is my Jolene dead?" Jimmy Lee's face scrunched up like he was about to cry.

Better get to it then. "We haven't gotten the DNA results back yet. But we have determined the woman's remains we found match the age and sex of Jolene Monroe. We found Jolene's purse with her credit card and driver's license beside the body. We're pretty sure it's her, Jimmy Lee. I'm sorry."

"But you're not sure?" He was grasping like any loved one would.

"Not a hundred percent. Not until we get the lab results back. That might take a while."

"Well, I won't believe it until you do."

"That's up to you, Jimmy Lee. But I want you to prepare yourself."

"Is that all you wanted to tell me?"

Mitch stared hard at the man, trying to ascertain his current mental state. Jimmy Lee had a history of mental illness and had been hospitalized several times in the past for it. "So, where have you been in the past months, Jimmy Lee?"

"Here and there. Off the grid." His body language didn't show that he was obviously lying, which was curious.

"Where? In Alabama? Georgia?"

"I don't have to tell you, do I? Are you charging me with a crime, Mr. Special Agent?"

"Have you committed one?"

"Nope."

"When was the last time you saw Jolene alive?" Mitch asked.

"When she left to drop off that dang dog of hers with the doc. Never saw her again. Maybe that's who you should ask."

"Who did she leave the dog with?" Mitch asked even though he knew.

"Bree Hawthorne, the therapist. That's why I'm here."

Mitch made a note like it was the first time he'd heard her name. His brain was having a hard time computing the facts right now. "Got it."

"That's who I came here to see. I wanted to ask if she'd seen Jolene again since she dropped off Tiny. Bree said Jolene'd brought some dog food and bones over after she'd dropped him off." Now it seemed he wanted to talk.

"When was this?" Mitch asked.

"I don't know. Ask her. She won't tell me anything."

"All right, Jimmy Lee. We'd like to keep in touch so we can let you know when we get those results back from the crime lab. Can you leave us a cell phone number or an address?"

Jimmy Lee shook his head. "Don't have one. Give me your card and I'll check in with you. How's that?"

"Fair enough." Mitch knew when to push and when not to. Jimmy Lee wanted to know what happened to his wife it seemed. Mitch didn't get the impression that he was the one responsible for her demise. Or maybe he wanted to find out what law enforcement knew. Either way, he seemed anxious to find out.

Mitch handed Jimmy Lee an official business card. "So, can you tell me how you met Bree Hawthorne?"

Jimmy Lee made a face. "Jolene wanted us to go to couples therapy, but I'd gone off my meds and Miz Hawthorne ended up calling 911 and sending me to the hospital because I was acting crazy in her office. Anyway, Jolene liked her and handed off her pup to the good doc while I was in the hospital. Things didn't go well, so she ended up leaving Tiny with her. Jolene loved that dog—but, uh she couldn't keep him when we left the hospital."

"Why couldn't she keep him?"

"The place we were at didn't allow dogs."

"What place was that?" Mitch asked.

"None of your damned business."

Mitch ignored Jimmy Lee's words. "Was it a motel? An apartment?"

"I got nothing else to say." Jimmy Lee crossed his arms and leaned back in his chair.

"All right. You give me a call in a couple of weeks if you want to find out what happened to Jolene. We should know something by then."

"Don't y'all follow me, you hear?"

"Should we follow you?" Mitch asked.

"Y'all leave me alone. I haven't done anything wrong." Jimmy Lee was getting agitated again.

Jimmy Lee picked up his hat that he'd placed on the table and set it atop his head, looked Mitch square in the eye, and said, "I don't believe she's dead." Then, he walked out. "And if it turns out that she is, I know who to blame."

"Who's that, Jimmy Lee?"

His expression darkened. "None of your business."

"Don't you want Jolene's killer brought to justice?"

"Oh, they'll be brought to justice. I'm the only one who knows how to do it too."

"Jimmy Lee, you don't want to end up in prison. Let us help."

Jimmy Lee shook his head. "Nope."

The deputy sitting outside the room stood and looked at Mitch questioningly. "Let him go."

Mitch joined Chase where he'd been observing the interviewing. "Should we put a car on him?" Chase asked. "I had one of the deputies put a tracker on his truck while y'all were chatting." Setting up manned surveillance took time and money, and so far they didn't have any hard evidence that Jimmy Lee was guilty of anything—especially murder.

"Good thinking." As Chase and Mitch walked toward the front, Mitch noticed Bree Hawthorne sitting in one of the chairs near the entrance, flipping through a *Garden and Gun* magazine. He got a tight little knot in the pit of his stomach. Nerves? He rarely got nervous about anything.

Mitch cleared his throat and Bree looked up.

"Well, hello, Special Agent Calloway. Nice to see you again." She flashed him that beauty pageant smile and he couldn't help being reminded of Dolly Parton. All that blonde hair and those white teeth. So pretty.

"Hello, Miz Hawthorne. Glad you're here. Seems we need to have a chat." He measured his words, careful to not say anything awkward, as he was often wont to do.

"Yes, it appears that we do." She looked over to where Chase was standing. "Did you want to do it here or at my office?" she asked.

"Up to you."

"LET'S HEAD OVER to my office, if you don't mind. It's a little more…cozy." Bree knew she hadn't done anything wrong—or she didn't think she had. But being questioned by these men on her own turf might be more comfortable for her and for Tiny, who was squirming a little.

The two men followed her down the sidewalk and she let them into her small refuge. It was comfortable and well decorated, with two good-sized tan leather chairs, a soft print upholstered sofa, and a smaller striped chair with wood trim where Bree normally sat. There was a rug, a coffee table, and long cream-colored curtain panels that framed the large windows overlooking the rear of the office that surprisingly had a tiny green space and a small tree outside the window.

"Welcome, gentlemen. Can I offer you coffee, tea, or water?"

Both men shook their heads at her offer. She pulled Tiny out of his carry bag and set him on his pillow. He stretched and yawned and settled.

"Is that Jolene Monroe's dog—Tiny?" Mitch Calloway asked. His voice sounded surprised.

"Yes, this is Tiny."

"Are you aware that we believe we've found Jolene Monroe's remains?"

"Chase said y'all found her but he didn't say she'd passed. But I assumed maybe she had. I didn't know she was officially missing until Jimmy Lee came by my office yesterday morning. He just showed up out of the blue after nearly two years."

"Bree, I need you to start from the beginning, if you don't mind. Please tell me how and when you first met Jimmy Lee and Jolene Monroe."

Bree took a deep breath and proceeded to fill Mitch and Chase in. She told them about Jimmy Lee's mental state the day they'd come in her office, how Jolene had asked her to take Tiny, and how she'd left Tiny and not come back. "I just assumed she'd come back and pick him up."

"At what point did you try and contact her regarding the dog?" Mitch asked.

"About two weeks after she'd left him. She'd filled out some paperwork, so I tried to call the number on the forms. It was no longer in service."

"Was there an address given on the paperwork?" he asked.

"I don't think so. They called last minute, and because I'd had a cancelation, I was able to fit them in. I usually go back over the paperwork before clients leave their first appointment but things got hectic and I had to call 911. Jimmy Lee—well, he was in a bad state. There should be hospital records with their information from that day."

"The information was bogus. The address didn't exist. Nor did the cell number."

"But didn't either of them have a job?" Bree asked.

"Jolene worked at a veterinary clinic, but nobody there knew where they were living before she quit."

"So, where's he been all this time? I mean, I guess we know now where Jolene's been."

"He says he's been off the grid."

Bree frowned. "Jolene dropped off a box with food and toys for Tiny a couple of weeks after their office visit and Jimmy Lee's hospital admittance. He wanted to see the note and to know exactly what was in the box she left. That's what we were discussing when Chase showed up this morning. He got agitated as soon as he read the note—like maybe there was something he'd missed with the box and the toys."

"Do you have the note?"

Bree nodded and walked over to where she'd placed it, picked it up, and handed it to Mitch. She caught a whiff of his aftershave. He smelled nice.

"What about the box?"

"It's at home in my closet. I haven't thought about it in a long time. I really don't remember much except that I'd taken the food out and a few of the toys. There might still be a couple of toys in there. I kind of shoved it aside. I'd gotten it when I was in the middle of my move from Huntsville, and I had a lot going on at the time." That was an understatement.

"Weren't you curious why she didn't come back?"

Bree lifted a shoulder. "I was. But I'd witnessed Jimmy Lee's temper and illness, and how hard it was for her to manage his condition at the time. And I also saw that he was unkind to Tiny. The poor little guy shook and whined like crazy around him. I believed that Jolene knew they weren't a good fit. She sacrificed her puppy to save her marriage. Or at least she believed that's what she was doing." Bree had been satisfied with Jolene's motives for leaving Tiny at the time.

"Did it occur to you that Jolene might be in trouble?" Mitch held her eyes in an intense stare.

Bree slowly shook her head. "No. It didn't. Or I didn't think so at the time. It was strange, yes. But I tend to let them go when they leave. My patients. It's hard when they won't let me help them." Bree broke eye contact. She refused to let him see her vulnerability. Because this was her soft spot. Momma didn't let her help. And Daddy left them.

"Thanks for your help, Bree." Chase stood, signaling that their meeting was over. Chase was a pretty sensitive guy, given that he didn't look like one. Mitch finally got a clue and followed suit.

"No problem. Please let me know if you find out anything else."

"I'll need to hang on to this note as evidence. Do you mind if I come and have a look at the box Jolene left with you for Tiny?" Mitch glanced over at the pup. And strangely, his stern expression softened. He actually smiled at Tiny.

"N-no, I don't mind. When do you want to stop by?"

"I'll be here for a while. What time do you get off work today?"

"Around five." Bree had three patients scheduled after lunch.

"Okay. I'll do some paperwork and make some phone calls at the sheriff's office until then. Can you meet me there after you're done here?" he asked.

Bree nodded. "Sure. I'll see you later."

Chapter Seven

BREE WAS FINISHING her patient notes when Mitch Calloway rang the bell out front. She kept the door locked while seeing patients so as not to be disturbed during therapy. When Jimmy Lee had come in yesterday, her workday hadn't yet started, so the door wasn't locked. From now on, she planned to keep it locked all the time.

As she opened the door for Mitch, she stepped back, once again admiring what a nice-looking man he was. Bree hadn't dated anyone since moving to Moonshine. She'd been so busy working that she hadn't been looking. Plus, it was kind of slim pickings in a town this small. Most of the men here were farmers and factory workers, and most were married to their high school sweethearts.

The more educated men lived and worked white-collar jobs either in Chattanooga or Atlanta over an hour away. Bree had decided that city life wasn't for her—not anymore. "Are you ready to go?" Mitch asked.

Bree nodded. "Just finishing up. Let me grab Tiny."

Mitch followed her to her back office where they'd chatted with Chase earlier today. "Do you mind?" He pointed toward Tiny before she'd had a chance to scoop him from his pillow bed.

Bree frowned, not exactly sure what he meant.

"Can I hold Tiny?"

"I-I'm not sure if he'll let you. He doesn't really like men." Truth was, Bree didn't let many people get near Tiny.

Mitch kind of turned and backed toward where Tiny sat. He inched closer without making eye contact with the pup and stood beside him as he eased his hand toward Tiny's side. Tiny didn't jump or whine. He leaned toward Mitch's hand and sniffed it. Then, he licked it. "Hey there, Tiny." Mitch spoke softly as he moved the back of his hand toward Tiny's head and stroked it. "Good to meet you, boy."

Tiny immediately flipped over for a belly rub, the little traitor, and proved Bree wrong. "Well, I'll be. He's not even shaking."

"I've got a way with animals. People, not so much."

"Honestly, Mitch, I haven't noticed that you struggle much doing your job." Bree was being truthful.

"I don't. I work on facts and evidence. It's the small talk that gets me in trouble." He continued rubbing Tiny's belly.

"Well, I'm finished here, so you can follow me to my house if you want."

"Any dinner plans?"

Bree shook her head. "I planned to heat up a can of soup, make cheese toast, and eat it out on my back deck with a glass of Pinot Noir. You are welcome to join me if you're hungry." It occurred to her that he probably was hungry. Guys always seemed to be hungry.

"Are you sure you wouldn't mind having a strange man over for dinner?"

"You're not so strange, Special Agent." Bree smiled at him.

He smiled back. "Then, I accept. Sorry, if I kind of forced the invite."

She waved her hand. "Nonsense."

"My car is just back there." She pointed behind the building. "Wait for me here and I'll pull around so you can follow me."

Mitch was parked in front in a designated space for the sheriff's office.

MITCH FOLLOWED BREE to her house out by Lake Blue Ridge about ten minutes outside of Moonshine. The dirt road wound and twisted until they ended up at the most picturesque little cabin he'd ever seen.

As she parked her car under the small carport, he pulled in behind her. The view of the water was incredible. "Wow, what a place."

"Thanks. I feel lucky to have found it when I moved here. The property values have increased quite a bit since then, so it was a good time to buy." She set Tiny down in the grass and he immediately did his business.

Mitch had been looking to buy a house for the last year or so and knew what she meant. The housing market had really exploded, even in the rural areas in Georgia recently. He figured it had something to do with everybody working from home since COVID and moving out of the city. "What a find."

She unlocked the front door and he was even more charmed by the interior. It was rustic but not masculine. The place had shiplap walls painted a cream instead of the usual dark wood, which added more light. The entire back wall was windows besides the fireplace and hearth. The kitchen was updated with light marble countertops and a big farmhouse sink and a huge gas range. "Do you like to cook?" he asked.

"Sometimes. But it's hard to cook for just one person. I entertain here and there, so I like to cook then. The kitchen was like this when I bought the place, so it comes in handy."

"It's very nice."

"Yes. I'm glad I didn't have to do any renovating." She deposited Tiny on his fluffy bed at the end of the comfy-looking sofa.

"I'll go and look for the box that Jolene brought by, if you want to look in the pantry and pull out a couple of cans of soup. The bread is on top of the microwave and the cheese and butter are in the fridge." She figured if he was eating, he could make himself useful in the kitchen.

"Got it. Any preference on what kind of soup? Looks like you've got at least three of every variety."

Bree laughed. The state of her pantry wasn't something she was proud of. She liked a neat-ish house, but Bree was a creative and didn't mind a little clutter here and there. "Surprise me."

She heard the sliding and stacking of cans. Was he organizing her canned goods? Her pantry might've just thrown his OCD into overdrive.

Bree opened the hallway closet where she last remembered seeing the box. Her jackets and coats hung inside, so she squatted down and moved aside two bins of Christmas decorations, a broken Roomba, and a rolled-up runner that Tiny had soiled twice before she'd decided to have it cleaned and remove the temptation.

Ah, there it was. It was relatively small, maybe fourteen by fourteen and around ten inches deep, and made of cardboard. It appeared to contain several puppy pads, a few colorful squeaky toys, a rawhide bone, and an extra-small halter/leash combo. Bree stood and carried it to the kitchen where Mitch appeared to have created a somewhat fancy meal from her humble ingredients.

"That was fast. Looks great." He'd found her Gruyère cheese and the multi-grain bread she'd saved in the freezer because it was too good to throw away. He'd selected the two chunky-style soups and heated them both together on the stove, whereas Bree would've certainly used the microwave. And he'd cut up strawberries and melon from the fridge and placed them in a bowl.

"No sense in behaving like animals." His smile was wide and stunning, reminding Bree that she hadn't been on a date with a man in a very long time.

"I'll get the wine and meet you at the high top outside." She nodded toward the box. "No sense doing this on an empty stomach."

"No wine for me. I'll just have water."

Bree nodded. She knew he was driving, but she respected anyone who chose not to drink for whatever reason.

He carried their food outside while she filled a glass with ice and water for him and grabbed the corked bottle of red on the counter she'd opened last night and a glass.

The sun was just starting to set as they settled in at the

small table. Bree had popped back inside to grab Tiny so he could hang out and chew on a turkey tendon on his favorite lounger while they ate. She would feed him later.

"This is nice. Thanks for hosting me."

"Of course. I couldn't let you go hungry." Purple and orange streaked across the sky and reflected on the water.

"Do you sit out here every night?" Mitch asked.

"Almost. It's my form of therapy." She took a deep breath and closed her eyes. "I take in a lot of other people's trauma every day. I try to let it go at the end of the day and not hang on to it too tightly."

"I know what you mean. I see a lot of trauma and abuse—and death. It tends to wear on you after a while."

Bree nodded. "I imagine our jobs are similar in a lot of ways. You mostly see it and I mostly hear about it." She sipped her wine and noticed the sky had changed from orange to gray and dark blue.

"It's a lot of both, I guess. I think about the murder victims a lot. What they saw, how they felt, and what they might have experienced. I do the same with the perpetrators. I try to get inside their heads. I feel like it helps me in solving cases."

Bree stared at Mitch. "Wow. I admire your dedication. Not everybody has that kind of empathy. It's rare."

"I feel like it takes an empath to know an empath—or at least that's what I've found in my experience."

Bree shrugged. "I guess that might be true. The road to becoming an empath is a tough one. It takes experiencing personal trauma to feel for others."

Mitch nodded. "Yes. It does."

"I'm sorry for whatever it was that you had to go through."

"Same." Despite the waning light, she could see the depth of meaning in his eyes. It appeared that the special agent had a complicated past.

They'd both finished eating by the time the sun finally set, leaving them in the dim shadow of dusk. "I guess we'd better head inside while we can still see."

Bree cleared their plates, and before she had the chance, Mitch scooped Tiny up like a football without any complaint from her little buddy and carried him inside along with his chewy.

She left the dishes in the sink and recorked the wine since she'd only had the one glass. That was her limit—it was a strict limit, and it was a challenge Bree had put upon herself since she'd been old enough to drink. One beer. Or one drink. Or one glass of wine. Any more than that might mean trouble. Her mother's alcoholism wasn't some kind of roulette she planned to mess around with in her life. She refused to invite in that kind of destruction.

Bree brought the box over to the ottoman in the living room and set it down where they could look through it carefully. She turned on the lamps and the overhead light to be sure nothing could be missed.

"I'LL NEED TO grab my evidence collection kit from the car. Be right back." Mitch decided that since the woman who'd dropped this with Bree was the victim of a murder, and since it might've been the last time she'd been placed at a scene, collecting any fingerprints, fibers, hair, or other evidence inside the box was prudent investigative procedure. He'd already bagged the note Bree had given him earlier and planned to drop it off at the lab for the forensics team to take a look at.

When he returned, he pulled on latex gloves, lifted the lid to get a glimpse of what was inside: a few plush toys, a rawhide chew toy, a dark green flannel blanket folded at the bottom. Bree stood just over his shoulder. She smelled nice. He wondered if he should tell her that, or if it would sound creepy. He never knew the right thing to say.

"What's that?" she asked, pointing.

There was a sliver of white that was barely discernible peeking out from underneath what looked like a piece of cardboard at the bottom of the box. He'd nearly missed it as there was a folded blanket that nearly covered it. Since Mitch had the latex gloves on, he carefully reached inside and gently tugged the edge of what was a white legal-sized envelope. It had the word INSURANCE carefully printed in block letters with a black permanent marker. The envelope was sealed, so Mitch wasn't going to open it here.

"Wonder what that could mean?" Bree asked in a whisper.

"Could mean a number of things. But I need to get it over to the crime lab and let them analyze it."

"Now I'm really curious. I can't believe this has been in my house all this time and I didn't pay attention to it. I was going through a lot of emotional stuff when Tiny came to me, and this box was the last thing on my mind."

He stared up at her, noticing how pretty her eyes were. "Don't beat yourself up, Bree. Sometimes the smallest thing can help solve a case. I'm just glad you thought about it being here now."

"I might never have given it another thought if Jimmy Lee hadn't shown up here."

Mitch was having a hard time concentrating on the subject at hand. He really wanted to kiss Bree. She was standing close to him and his body was reacting to her in a way that he'd not felt toward a woman in a very long time. So, he said, "We had Jimmy Lee tracked with traffic cameras to an approximate area. We should be able to find him if we need to."

He was such an idiot with women. And he so wanted not to be with Bree Hawthorne.

"Can you keep me posted on what's inside the envelope?" Bree asked as she followed Mitch to his car.

"I'll tell you what I can. Might have some additional questions for you once we get the evidence results back. If we don't find anything, I'll return it to you. Technically, it belongs to you." It would give him a reason to see her again soon. He wished he could be more open about the evidence with her, but unless she was officially looped in as a professional on the investigation, he would need to keep the information within the bounds of law enforcement.

Bree nodded. "Okay. Well, don't be a stranger, Special Agent."

"It was nice to see you again, Bree. Thanks again for dinner."

"You're very welcome, Mitch."

The way she said his name sent a chill down his spine— in a good way. He put the box inside the trunk of this car and said goodbye, wishing there was a good way to ask to see her again. "Tell Tiny I'll see him soon."

"Will do." She smiled at him when she said it. Maybe like she knew he was looking for something clever to say and was too kind to make him feel like the dud he was.

Mitch forced himself to concentrate on the case. Plus, he might have just gotten a break. He could hardly wait to get this new evidence processed by forensics to see what was in the envelope. Insurance could mean pet insurance for Tiny. Especially since she worked for a veterinarian. Or it could mean insurance in case something happened to her. A way to make sure that if it did, somebody would be held accountable.

Mitch had seen it a lot over the years. People often knew when they were in danger. And sometimes they left clues— just in case.

Chapter Eight

B REE WATCHED MITCH drive off, wondering if he'd gotten the hint that she liked him. She'd all but made kissy faces at him and begged him to call her. Yes, he was focused on the case—as was she. But it was obvious that he didn't take hints well. It was probably due to his Asperger's. Hints weren't the best form of communication with those on the autism spectrum. Bree realized she might have to be a bit more direct if she wanted to get his attention.

She did think that he liked her. But it was going to be up to her to be a little more direct in her communication with him. He was charming in his way and she appreciated that he appeared to be a straight arrow. Mitch believed in following the rules and wouldn't tell her anything he shouldn't about the investigation. It was annoyingly admirable.

But the curiosity was killing her.

Having dinner on the deck with Mitch had been nice—more than nice. They'd *almost* talked about themselves. Bree never talked about herself. Her past. Not with anyone besides her sister. She'd gotten the impression that Mitch might have a similarly *interesting* story to tell. Not just about how he'd managed to become successful and confident despite his autism. That in itself was pretty amazing, Bree knew. She knew because she regularly worked with patients who dealt with the challenges of it.

Bree could feel a kindred haunted soul in Mitch. The deep sadness. The loss. He'd suffered. Yet, she could also tell that he still had hope for a better life beyond it. She was able to tell those who'd lost their hope. It was her superpower. Not a great one to have, but it was nice to know what she was dealing with. Hope was the seed she could work with. Without it, the road to recovering a fulfilled life was dismal and unlikely.

Returning to the sofa with Tiny, Bree thought about her past and her childhood. How Daddy had abandoned Momma at her lowest point, and how he'd abandoned two little girls who needed him. What kind of man removed his support, both emotional and physical, not to mention financial, from his completely helpless family? The old rage boiled up unexpectedly, and Bree pulled out her laptop. For years, she and Darla had made a pact not to search for him. Because to search for him made them seem needful of him. Bree wasn't sure if Darla had looked online for Daddy, but up until now, Bree hadn't.

Bree didn't need him. But now she wanted to know where her piece-of-shit daddy had gone to get away from his family. Had he started a family with another woman? Did she and Darla have siblings? Had he ever legally divorced Momma?

Bree was antsy, bored, and needed something to do with her mind. Sitting out here alone by the lake waiting to hear what happened to Jolene had lit a fire in her. Maybe it was Mitch who had lit that fire. Whatever it was, she needed to put her mind to work tonight. A thorough internet search for her missing father might be just the thing. Maybe he was dead. That would be the simplest thing. But when had anything with her family ever been simple?

She typed his name in a Google search: Bernard Hawthorne. She had no idea that was such a popular name. Doctors, lawyers, preachers. So many to choose from. Bree narrowed the search down to Alabama. That helped. But nothing she could use. Still not anyone who might be their daddy. He wasn't a real estate agent for sure, or a podiatrist. There were those nebulous listings that asked for a credit card to get the information, but she wasn't doing that. Bree snapped her laptop shut. Maybe she would ask Chase if he could do a search.

She sighed. Picking up her phone, she called Darla.

"Hey there. I was just thinking about you. What are you up to?" Hearing Darla's voice was like a balm to Bree's soul.

"I tried to find Daddy on the internet." Bree whooshed out the words on a breath. She felt guilty about it and hoped Darla wouldn't be angry with her.

"Honey. Why on earth would you do that? We agreed not to." Darla didn't really sound mad, just curious.

"Have you ever done it?" Bree asked her sister, not believing that she hadn't.

There was a brief silence. "Once. But I didn't find him. Who knew there were so many Bernard Hawthornes?"

"Right? It's a stupid name, anyway." Bree laughed. "I was just sitting here thinking about Momma, and how sad she was after Daddy left. Part of me wants to find him and let him have it."

"He deserves a lot more than a piece of your mind," Darla said. "I do hope that karma has found him and worked him over good, don't you?"

"Yes, I guess so." Bree so hoped so.

"I hope that he got married again to a younger woman and had a baby, and that his young wife made him babysit while she went out and spent all of his money and then left him to raise the baby alone." Darla said it with such relish that Bree grinned.

She pictured Darla's scenario. "I wish that on Daddy, but I wouldn't wish that on an innocent baby. Plus, that would be our sibling."

"Hmm. I hadn't thought about that."

"I guess I just wish that he regretted leaving us. That he's missed us every day of his life and sees our sad faces every time he closes his eyes at night. But that's my childhood fantasy. Maybe, I just wish that he has a bad case of gout and an STD that burns and won't go away."

Darla started laughing. "O-oh, that's so good. A-and maybe a hemorrhoid to go with it." She squealed with laughter.

"Don't strain your bladder over there, sister." But Bree was laughing almost as hard as Darla, picturing their very selfish father limping with gout and howling in pain when he peed and pooped.

"I'm so glad you called. And I'm glad you finally opened the can of worms too. I wonder about him all the time. I mostly hope he just up and died because then it would all be over."

Bree tended to agree. "Yes, but he would only be in his

early sixties. That's pretty young to die these days unless he's had an accident or cancer or something."

"I guess."

"I might ask somebody in law enforcement if they'll check to see where he is. If we really want to know. Do we really want to know?" Bree was suddenly serious.

"I'm not sure, Bree. I don't know what I'd do with that information."

"Me neither. Let's think about it and circle back, okay?"

"Okay."

MITCH WAS AT the lab first thing the next morning, despite the fact that it was raining cats and dogs outside. Georgia's hot summers often meant thunderstorms. He'd grabbed a raincoat and an umbrella and placed the box from Bree's house in a large garbage bag and sealed it. He included the earlier note in a separate plastic bag.

If the lab folks were surprised to see him, they hid it well. It wasn't the first time he'd shown up early with evidence demanding that they drop everything and process it. "I just collected this last night and it might be our break in this murder case."

"We'll get to it." He was handed a label and a bigger box. There were lockers for incoming evidence. "Put it in the locker for your case."

"C'mon, Clark. Don't make me light a fire on this one." Mitch wasn't exactly patient when it came to his evidence.

"We're slammed, over here, Mitch. I'm processing evidence from a murder scene that happened last night. It's fresh. There's blood and fluids. It's open and shut. We should be able to get to yours after lunch."

Mitch did notice that things were hopping in the lab, and that there were several extra forensics techs on duty this morning. "Okay. Let me know as soon as you get started on it." Mitch knew he could sound like an asshole from time to time, and he also knew that people could only do what they could, given what they had to work with.

"Will do." Clark didn't appear to be too annoyed with him. The two men had worked together on many cases over the last decade, so Mitch didn't want to leave on a bad note.

"Thanks, man. I appreciate it."

Clark nodded and immediately went back to what he'd been doing.

Mitch figured he had at least until after lunch before he found out anything about the contents of the box he'd gotten from Bree's house, so he left the crime lab and went back to his office, intent on shaking something out on this case.

Once he'd gotten settled at his desk, Mitch accessed the GPS log of Jimmy Lee's journey after leaving Moonshine yesterday. Fortunately, he was able to map Jimmy Lee's route from the sheriff's office in town and headed east of McCaysville, Georgia, near the Tennessee state line. Once Jimmy Lee got off of the state highway, it was hard to tell where he'd gone. The elevation was mountainous and the area was sparsely populated. Mitch now believed Jimmy Lee when he said he was off the grid. There were occasional blips where the GPS grabbed a signal here and there, so he had enough information to maybe find Jimmy Lee if necessary.

There weren't any real roads in that area, and it would take some real off-road SUVs to even contemplate getting out there. Even with Jimmy Lee's big tires, Mitch wondered about navigating that area. He'd need to do a deep dive to see who owned the land in the area—if it was state, federal, or privately held. Each held their own challenges when it came to investigating. Private land was the hardest as far as jumping through hoops to investigate.

Folks who lived that far out in the middle of nowhere didn't usually want anybody treading on their rights or their land. Mitch could envision Jimmy Lee as one of those kinds of folks on the one hand. On the other, he didn't really seem the type to go completely without social contact. He appeared to be showered, recently shaven, and his clothes were pretty clean. Mitch's experience with the off-the-grid folks had been that they were less—hygienic.

Mitch rubbed his eyes. Staring at his computer screen for hours at a time was a bad habit he'd gotten into when researching evidence. He looked at the time. Almost one o'clock. No wonder he was feeling hungry. Hopefully, he'd hear something about the evidence in the next couple of hours.

BREE'S LAST PATIENT before lunch was one of her very best friends in Moonshine, and one of the town's most famous residents. Sadie Brubaker Blackburn disappeared without a trace when she was sixteen, and for years everybody had wondered what had happened to her. On a fine spring day last year, she showed back up out of the clear blue. But Sadie had no memory of her childhood or the events that had led up to her disappearance. Bree had worked with Sadie as she regained her memory—and helped her with a lot of the fallout from the trauma of her past.

Sadie continued to come in and talk through some of the angst she still held toward both her momma and her step-mom, Thelma. Sadie was married to Chase Blackburn, Moonshine's sheriff.

Tiny sat on Sadie's lap as she stroked his head. Sadie was one of the very few people that Tiny trusted completely. Bree knew that if she ever needed a place for Tiny to stay, it would be with Sadie and her beagle mix, Daisy Mae. The two dogs loved each other.

"Have you read all of Thelma's journal yet?" Bree asked.

"I'm getting through it a little at a time. It's very emotional for me to learn about her life before we met. To know that she lived as an entirely different person back then and to learn all about it this way. She never told me anything." Thelma was Sadie's aunt who'd taken care of her after she'd left Moonshine as a teen. But Thelma hadn't been honest with Sadie, and Sadie hadn't found out the truth until after Thelma had died.

"I imagine that must be such a frustrating thing. I'm hoping that by the time you get to the end of it, it will give you some comfort." Thelma had left Sadie a journal after she'd died—a kind of guidebook that would help Sadie to understand things better.

Sadie looked at her watch. "Looks like it's time for lunch."

Bree laughed. "You're right." The two women always had lunch after Sadie's appointment. Today, they were meeting Jenny, Sadie's best friend who'd moved from Nebraska with her husband and new baby to Moonshine.

"Jenny's meeting us at the diner with Jeremy. She'll get a table."

"I can't wait to see that sweet angel again. How are they settling in?" Bree asked as she took Tiny from Sadie and tucked him in her bag.

"I've never seen anybody embrace a place like the two of them have Moonshine. It's like they wake up every morning at Disneyland. They absolutely love it here."

"Well, I guess they did come from Nebraska." Bree said this with a smile.

"True enough. But I came here from Nebraska and I've got some lovely memories from living there with Thelma. Some people just take to the South, I think."

They chatted as they strolled toward the diner, nodding and waving toward people they knew along the way. You couldn't swing a cat without hitting somebody you knew in a town like Moonshine. Plus, it was lunchtime, and just like in an elementary school when the bell rang and class let out, the people were everywhere at that time of the day.

As soon as they entered the diner, Jenny called out to them from a booth in the back to get their attention. Baby Jeremy was dressed all in green and snuggled tightly in his car seat sucking happily on his pacifier. "He gets cuter every time I see him, Jenny. Thanks for meeting us."

Jenny stood and hugged Bree as if they were old friends. They had become fast friends. Easy friends. Jenny Harris was not only Sadie's bestie from Nebraska, but she was also a therapist like Bree. She'd been Sadie's friend from college and had been fascinated by Sadie's memory loss. The two women had bonded and become like family over the years, along with Thelma. When Thelma died, they'd had each other.

"I'm thrilled this worked out. And I'm super thrilled to get out of the house and see other grown-ups. Jared is great, but he's getting on my nerves. You'd think the man had birthed Jeremy. He has so many *opinions*."

"Let me know when you want to get back to work even part time, Jenny. Hospital staff is getting serious about the idea of hiring another therapist pretty soon. I've got all the work I can handle here." They'd discussed the possibility of Jenny joining the hospital staff the last time they'd seen each other.

"Ah, that would be fantastic. I've started working on my licensing reciprocity paperwork, and things are moving along. I'll talk with Jared about it tonight. He's stay-at-home dad material if I've ever seen it. He talks about it all the time."

"Wow. That sounds kind of perfect really," Sadie said. Jared was an accountant turned glass artist, who'd realized his dream, and now worked in an old barn on their property out back of their house. Moonshine was the perfect town for artists of all types. There were so many galleries and festivals in the area and in the North Georgia mountain region in particular. So far, Jared had placed pieces in several galleries and worked hard to keep up with supply.

"Yes. We'd have to work out schedules. He spends a lot

of time out in the barn with very hot kilns and such. Not exactly baby-friendly stuff. He would need to get on a very tight working schedule, and he's an artist. Not exactly somebody who punches a clock these days."

"Are you okay leaving little Jeremy all day, Jenny?" Sadie asked.

"Of course I'm not. But I'm losing myself, Sadie. I need to help other people solve their problems. It's how I feel successful. Being a mommy is great, but I need more right now. Jared's greatest wish is to stay home and be Jeremy's primary parent."

"Sounds like the two of you just need to work out the particulars." Bree had counseled countless couples regarding this very thing. It was important to feel fulfilled, and to know that one's child was getting what they needed. A delicate balance indeed.

Bree found herself thinking about what it must be like to have a child and a husband. These women had both found love at around the same age Bree was now. She'd pretty much given up on the idea, but what if a family might still be around the next corner for her? Maybe she shouldn't be so content with living alone—being alone so much of the time.

A picture of Mitch Calloway flashed through her mind. Those serious gray eyes. He stirred something in her that hadn't been stirred in a long time. And she had a strong feeling that it was mutual. But with a guy like Mitch, it was hard to tell.

She wondered when she would hear from him again.

Chapter Nine

A ROUND THREE O'CLOCK, Mitch got a call from Clark at the lab. They were processing the evidence Mitch had brought in that morning and Clark wanted to show him something. Mitch had been sitting at his desk doing some paperwork and waiting for the phone to ring.

Mitch hoped nobody saw him run that yellow traffic light as he'd gotten to the lab in record time. It was highly frowned upon by management when agents broke the laws they were tasked to uphold and protect. He intentionally took a deep breath and slowed his roll as he walked from the parking lot to the front door, showed his badge to security, and made his way to where Clark was working through the evidence.

The box, along with the evidence found inside, was spread out on a large table. Each item was tagged and had been dusted for fingerprints and photographed. Clark was in the process of looking at something through a microscope. "Did you find something?" Mitch asked.

"Hmm. Maybe. Pull on a pair of gloves and read that letter over there." He pointed to a sheet of paper encased in a clear plastic bag. Mitch recognized the handwriting immediately as belonging to Jolene Monroe, as it was identical to the note she'd left Bree, which was also displayed with the other items.

The note read:

This is meant to be my insurance in case anything happens to me. I'm out here in the middle of nowhere with Jimmy Lee and his momma, Glynnis. We've joined some kind of "nature camp" that's supposed to be helpful in reducing our dependency on the outside world. It's called the Community of Atonement. It's supposed to help Jimmy Lee with his mental imbalance. (That's what his momma says, but I'm not so sure.) They've taken our keys and our valuables and locked them away. There's a man with a gun at the gate to "protect" us. The guru here calls herself Sarah. She and Glynnis seem to know each other and are tight. I'm pretty sure Glynnis wants us here so she can keep an eye on Jimmy Lee. There's a man they keep talking about who must be the head dude, but I haven't caught his name yet. He's not here and we haven't seen him yet. The people here seem to be wealthy folks who've "escaped" corporate jobs in the city. Some of them are complaining that Sarah won't allow them to call their families or let them leave. She tells them they haven't completed the program yet, and when they do, they won't want to reach out to people outside of the "sanctuary."

Just so you know, this is a bona fide cult we're mixed up in here. I was only able to leave because I was on a grocery outing with a young girl that I paid to keep quiet. I doubt I'll be able to do this again. I'm including the GPS location of where we are. I overheard Glynnis talking with Sarah about stealing money from the members here. So, I guess my mother-in-law is more than a bitch—she's a thug. A couple of the more complaining members have disappeared. We were told they left of their own accord. They might be buried with the compost they're so proud of. Who knows? Maybe they ran away, but I fear for our safety.

If you find this, please know that we are not in a good place. I didn't go to the police because I couldn't leave Jimmy Lee there alone and I was afraid we might have been followed.

Here's hoping you find this sooner rather than later,

Bree

Mitch's stomach seized up. Bree hadn't found it, and two years had passed. And Jolene was dead. Bree was an empathetic person, and it would really hurt her. He realized then that the very last thing he wanted to do was hurt Bree. But he couldn't keep it from her either.

Right now, he had to figure out how much more to all of this there might be than a single dead woman. This obviously involved a cult. It certainly wasn't the first to operate in the North Georgia mountain region. With the topography here, historically, the area had had its share of both religious and non-religious groups who'd operated in compounds over the years without discovery. Mitch shivered unexpectedly. He hated cults and how they preyed on the most vulnerable of people. He'd never met a cult leader with good intentions no matter how much they claimed to have them. It was always about power and control. Mitch realized it was now essential that they find Jimmy Lee. He wondered if that's where he'd been all this time. Was he still involved with the Community of Atonement? Or had he managed to get out? Where was his momma now? Where was Sarah? And the strange man in charge?

There were so many questions attacking Mitch's brain as the truth sunk in. He turned to Clark after rereading the letter from Jolene again. "We're gonna need a task force."

"Looks that way."

The area where the tracker they'd put on Jimmy Lee's truck had pinged within the border of Whitfield County, still within the same county as Moonshine. That meant it was Chase Blackburn's jurisdiction, which was good news. Chase was already dialed in on the case and could work with them to help locate Jimmy Lee and possibly the Community of Atonement, whatever they were. First, he'd need to call his supervisory agent in charge.

Cults required highly specialized investigations. Depending what kind of belief system the group operated under—religious, satanic, or nature-based—they had to be handled carefully. Most often, a group who separated itself from the rest of the world practiced things not accepted in regular society. They'd need to get an expert involved. Cults usually included entire families, so children were frequently endangered within the confines of the compound. When law enforcement approached, it could invariably put innocent lives at risk. These people were often willing to die for their causes.

Mitch took photos of the letter from Jolene to Bree. This was a huge break in the case, despite how upsetting it would be to Bree. He had a lot of work to do.

BREE NOTICED MITCH'S truck parked in front of the sheriff's office immediately when she locked up from seeing her last patient. Today was an early day, so she'd put Tiny in his stroller, and they were planning to get some sunshine and grab an ice cream cone—a pup cone for Tiny. The weather was hot and humid after the rain they'd had the last couple of days. But now, she was curious as to what Mitch was doing back in town. After all, he'd taken the stuff from her house and brought it to the lab for analysis. It would be good manners to at least fill her in as best he could. And maybe she was just a little bit salty that he hadn't let her know, or asked if she'd like to have lunch, or maybe grab a coffee—or something.

Well, she *did* have to pass by the sheriff's office to get to the ice cream place, didn't she? Just as she approached the door to the office, Randy Slade strode up the sidewalk. He nodded toward her and said, "Hi, Bree. You're just the person I was coming to speak to. The GBI might need your help. Have you had any experience in dealing with cults?"

Bree stared at him as if he'd grown another set of eyeballs. "Cults? Uh, yes, I've had some experience with them. I did a special study during my clinical rotation on cult behavior."

"I told Chase and Mitch on the phone that you were our girl on this one." He opened the door to Chase's office and motioned for Bree to step inside. "Do you mind? We're about to have a meeting."

Bree frowned. "I haven't heard anything about this yet."

"It just came up this morning. The GBI is putting together a task force. Looks like Jolene got herself mixed up with a cult up here in the mountains. Now, we've gotta find Jimmy Lee and get some answers."

Bree's eyes widened. *Oh, no.* Mitch must've learned something from the letter he found inside the box at her house. Something about a cult.

Bree adjusted her eyes from the bright sunshine outside to the fluorescent lighting of the sheriff's office. "Hey there, Bree," Hannah called from her desk.

"Oh, hi, Hannah." She waved.

"Is that Tiny you've got there in the stroller?"

"Yes. We were headed out for ice cream when Randy caught us and rerouted us here."

Mitch stepped toward her. "I'm glad he caught you, Bree. I need to fill you in on some important new information."

"I'm guessing it's about the letter we found in the box?" Bree asked.

He nodded. "It's a doozy."

She noticed he was wearing jeans today. That was a first. Of course, he had on a button-up shirt and a sport jacket over it, but still, for him that was as casual as she'd seen him. Something must've really thrown him off his routine. But she kind of liked seeing Mitch a little disheveled. It was sexy. "I'm all ears."

"We're waiting for my boss to arrive, along with the state police captain."

Bree frowned. "What on earth is happening?"

"We've uncovered something with the potential to be a

lot bigger than just a single murder. It appears to have cult involvement."

"Randy mentioned you might need a consult. I did a specialized study of cults and cult culture and behavior. I can help with the profile if you need me to." Part of her dreaded delving deep into the whole cult thing because of her own strange past. The "church" that took them in when she was a child was more cult than church, and as an adult looking back, she realized how harmful they were to her family—mostly to Momma. But maybe to Daddy as well. He seemed to really absorb their treatment of Momma as justice for her sins. He'd treated her far differently after their time there.

"I didn't realize you had experience in this area. It's a relief, really. I wanted to tell you about what we found out but didn't want to break protocol. If we can pull you in as a special consultant on the case, we'll be able to discuss the details of the case freely."

"This isn't my first rodeo, Mitch. I've worked with the GBI, the sheriff's department, and the state police to help with profiling in cases previously."

"Yes, I remember you've said so."

Bree could tell he still didn't take her seriously as a partner in solving crime, but that was okay for now. She would see how things evolved moving forward. Knowing that he faced challenges socially was one thing. Being treated by him as someone who had a lesser brain was another. Time would tell which was at play here.

Before either of them had the chance to say anything else, the door opened and several dark-suit-wearing law enforcement agents filed inside. There were two women and at least six men. To say the place filled up in an instant was a drastic understatement.

Chase cleared his throat. "Excuse me. We've got a developing situation, everyone. Let's get started. I'll let Special Agent Roberts open things up."

"Thanks, Sheriff Blackburn. I'm the special agent in charge, Aaron Roberts, from the Atlanta field office of the GBI. It's come to our attention this morning that we've got a possible cult situation operating in the northwest corner of Whitfield County, approximately fifteen miles due east of Moonshine in a particularly mountainous area. We are putting together a profile of the group to see what type of individuals we are dealing with, and how many are involved. Remains of a woman were discovered that tie the cult to a homicide over near Dalton. Evidence was uncovered in the last twenty-four hours that suggests the cult have been holding members against their will and there might be other homicide victims. We've got a lot to parse out here to determine the best way forward. It's going to take some time, so we appreciate your patience. If you have any information on a group called the Community of Atonement, please bring it to Special Agent Mitch Calloway. Special Agent Calloway will be running point on this one.

"We're setting up a task force to research the group and develop our plan of attack. Sheriff Blackburn has graciously agreed to host us in his office for now until we can find roomier accommodations. We'll be using the conference room in back as a headquarters starting today. Grab a desk, a chair, a corner, or a bench or shady spot outside in the town square. The diner across the street serves good food, is air-conditioned, and open all day. Be polite and don't forget to tip your server."

Bree was shocked at the lightning-fast response to what they'd found in Jolene's letter. She turned to Mitch. "I guess I'm a part of this now since I've just been part of the debriefing."

Mitch nodded. "Let me introduce you to my boss and get you officially looped into the case. There'll be papers to sign, of course."

"Of course."

Bree's mind immediately started clicking. She'd need to call Sadie's friend, Jenny Harris, right away. Bree's schedule was pretty tight, but she started work around eight thirty in the morning and left work by five most days. So, her days were fairly reasonable. No late nights or call unless one of her patients was suicidal.

Currently, she didn't have any patients who were at risk of suicide or hospitalized, so that was a relief. She and Jenny could discuss the support groups. Jenny was an old pro and Bree believed that she could more than handle sliding into Bree's role temporarily. Patients like Ralph Barnes, who mostly complained that his wife was too fat, might just want to take a break from therapy until Bree came back to the office.

"Sir, this is Bree Hawthorne. She's a clinical therapist and has had some additional training in cult behavior. Her practice is two doors down. We'd like to pull her in on the case as a consultant and profiler."

Bree realized she was face-to-face with the special agent in charge. "Pleasure to meet you, Dr. Hawthorne." He stuck out his hand in greeting.

"Just Bree is fine." She didn't usually use her PhD title with other professionals. "It's nice to meet you."

"Thanks for your willingness to help us out on this one. I think I remember you. Didn't you give us a hand a year or so ago on that kidnapping case in Atlanta?" he asked.

Bree nodded. "Yes. Glad we were able to find the child in time."

"Mostly thanks to your insight. Happy to have you on board. I'll have my assistant send over some documents for your signature. Same as last time."

"Great. I hope I can help."

Mitch had been watching the interaction and Bree noticed a gleam of something in his eyes. Admiration? "Looks like we'll be working together? How's that going to work with your schedule?"

"I've got someone in mind who can cover most of my patients. I just spoke with her yesterday and she's eager to get back to work after having a baby."

"Sounds good. So, I want to show you Jolene's letter, but please understand that there's nothing you could've done differently." His very serious expression was back.

"O-okay."

He pulled something up on his phone. "Here's the screenshot."

She read the letter—twice. And Mitch was right to have warned her. It was a real punch in the gut. If only she'd paid more attention back then. "How awful."

"You couldn't have known, Bree."

Bree shook her head. "No, I couldn't have. It was a bad

time for me. I was very distracted." She could tell that he wanted to ask her more about it, but someone approached them.

"Special agent Calloway?" a young deputy asked. "I'm Sean Davis with the Moonshine Sheriff's department. I think I've heard of the group y'all were talking about. I don't know much, but somebody at a convenience store outside of town was talking about a group of people living up in the hills yonder and how they live off the land and spin yarn from sheep's wool. Said they send somebody into town once a month to get groceries and supplies. Stopped for gas at their store. They called it a nature camp. That's all I heard, but I thought I would let you know."

"That's good information, Deputy. Where did you say the store was? What's it called?" Mitch took down the information on a notepad while Bree reread the letter again.

Bree realized then how much her life was about to change, at least temporarily. Her first plan of action was to contact Jenny. Then, she could see about signing paperwork to help out with this case. Her patients had to come first. Once they were covered, she could move forward to assist in finding out who killed Jolene. She owed the poor woman that much.

Chapter Ten

B REE WALKED WITH Tiny down to her office and contacted Jenny just minutes after she left Mitch at Chase's office amidst what felt like chaos. Since Mitch was running point on the investigation, Bree knew that he would be busier than a one-armed paper hanger in the coming days. But at least Bree would know what was happening, and hopefully they would see each other regularly.

She moved Tiny from the stroller to his pillow so he would be comfortable while she made her phone calls and got to work on getting things in order so that she could focus on helping with the case.

Jenny was surprised to hear from Bree so soon after they'd met for lunch and seemed thrilled to have the opportunity to jump back into working a regular schedule. "I can come in tomorrow if that works for you, and we can go through patient charts."

"I'll have the patients for tomorrow come in for their scheduled appointments, and I'll introduce you to them and they can decide if they want to temporarily suspend therapy or continue with their appointments already on my book. We can do the same for the next couple of days until most of the regulars have met you. I'll call the ones we miss and speak with them about the temporary changes so they can make their decision."

"That sounds perfect. What about the hospital support groups?" she asked.

"I'll speak with my supervisor at the hospital today. How far along are you on the licensure reciprocity procedures?" Jenny had briefly mentioned this at lunch.

"I've been approved already for licensure by endorsement because my qualifications meet the Georgia standards, but I'll still need to sit for the oral and jurisprudence exams. I've got those scheduled for next month. I hope that won't be a problem."

Bree was thrilled that Jenny was this far along on these important steps, showing that she'd been serious about returning to work soon. "I'll know more later today. Worst case, there might be some things you won't be able to do until after the exams. You should be able to do family counseling and group sessions at the hospital. There is a psychiatrist who comes in twice a month. Maybe he can take the patients who require clinical therapy."

"I've been doing this work for over a decade. It seems silly that because I moved to a different region, suddenly I'm not qualified."

"It's bureaucracy for sure. Every state thinks their re-quirements are the most stringent and will keep the standards high."

"Definitely want to keep out the psychology riff-raff." Jenny half-laughed.

"Something like that. Hopefully, it won't be an issue. But mostly I do family therapy in the office. The more serious cases usually come to me through the hospital."

The last time Bree had helped law enforcement with the kidnapping case in Atlanta, the hospital had brought in someone temporarily from Atlanta and they'd worked out of the hospital. Since it was only for a couple of weeks and she'd had fewer patients then, she'd paused her patients and still saw a few here and there since she was working mostly remotely with the GBI and the FBI giving profiling expertise.

This felt bigger. Like the scope of things and people involved was going to be more expansive. Bree got the impression it would take up a lot more of her time and energy. Hopefully, she would be able to keep Tiny with her while she worked. If they planned to center the operations here in Moonshine, she should be able to.

Bree made an appointment immediately to speak with her supervisor, Dr. Sonny McNeal, at the hospital. He appreciated that her education and experience was sought for important cases by law enforcement. It brought the hospital good media. Good media enhanced the reputation of the hospital. For a small hospital like Moonshine General, that shared patients with other regional healthcare centers, it made a huge difference financially when patients chose their facility over another about the same distance from home. So, when Bree needed to be away for short periods, Dr. McNeal usually helped her work it out.

Today was no exception. She'd gotten a last-minute in-person meeting with Dr. McNeal, so she grabbed Tiny and settled him in his carry bag after letting him out to walk around on his leash for a few minutes outside her office.

"You say that Dr. Harris has equivalent credentials from Nebraska and is in the process of licensure reciprocity?"

"Yes. She's pretty far along in the process." Bree repeated what Jenny had told her.

"If she's already been endorsed by the state board, then the rest is mostly red tape. I'll speak with my contact on the state board and make sure there isn't an issue. We're very proud of the work you do, Bree. You shine a light on our little hospital, which brings in more patients. More patients bring more revenue. As much as we care about our community, we are a business, and the parent company appreciates success. So, you do what needs doing, and we'll take your word that Dr. Harris can manage things in the interim. Of course, we'll do our usual background check and vet her as well."

"Of course. I appreciate your giving her the opportunity. She did some good work with Sadie Brubaker. Dr. Harris was Sadie's therapist and friend back in Nebraska where she lived before coming back to Moonshine. She and I collaborated on Sadie's case, which allowed her to be cleared of any wrongdoing."

"Ah, our famous Sadie Brubaker. That's certainly a feather in her cap then."

BREE LEFT THE hospital feeling positive about the transition for Jenny to take over for her temporarily now that Dr. McNeal was on board. He would pave the way for a smooth changeover.

She made her way back to the sheriff's office where Mitch was still hard at work. He'd shed his jacket and rolled up his sleeves. He was sitting at a desk in the corner of the large office with papers and files spread out around him. "They didn't want you in the conference room with the suits?" Bree asked as she approached with Tiny in her bag.

Mitch shook his head. His eyes were a little droopy. "I don't work well sitting around with a bunch of other people. I do best with my own space. I need to be able to look at things and think."

Bree nodded. "Makes sense. Any new information?"

"Our first priority is to find Jimmy Lee. We put a tracker on his truck when he was here yesterday, but he's in a hard-to-reach area and the signal is in and out. They're putting together an off-road team to head out there now."

"What if he's on cult property?"

"It's a possibility but we don't think so. Jolene's letter intimated that members weren't able to come and go as they pleased. Jimmy Lee gave us the impression that he's living on his own, but the team will be stealthy and prepared just in case. They'll send up a drone first to get an idea of what we're dealing with. We think Jimmy Lee has most of the inside information since he's lived in the confines of the compound. He should know how many members there are, how well armed they are, and what daily life looks like there."

"Sounds like it. He'd been there with Jolene, and it sounds like his momma was in cahoots with the cult leader, Sarah. It also sounded like he blames them for her disappearance and murder—if that's who he was referring to when he said he knew who was to blame if Jolene is dead."

"Is there a question that Jolene is dead?" Bree asked.

Mitch shook his head. "No, not really. The lab is backed up on getting DNA results, but all of the physical evidence suggests that the remains are Jolene's. Unless we discover something otherwise, we are working under that assumption. Plus, nobody's seen or heard from her since the day she dropped off the box for Tiny at your house. That's pretty compelling evidence right there."

"I'd have to agree."

"It's a strange dynamic for his momma to be involved, don't you think?" Mitch asked, changing the subject rapidly. She could see that he was ticking off a checklist in his brain. His process. Everybody had a method to sift through their thoughts. Mitch was a very interesting person to Bree. Aside from being attractive physically, he was a fascinating case study.

Bree had to be careful with someone like Mitch. She could feel herself being drawn to him not only as an interesting person, but also as a man. After how badly she'd been hurt by Doug, she had to stay a step back and keep things friendly but still professional.

"Very Freudian for sure."

"It makes you wonder about the relationship between Jimmy Lee's momma and Jolene. Jimmy Lee has a lot of explaining to do when we find him. I just hope we can get him out of his hole without a problem. First we have to locate him."

"Have you eaten yet today?" Bree asked.

Mitch looked up. "Uh, no. I don't think so. Just a protein shake this morning on the way out."

"Can you take a break and grab something? It's pretty important that you maintain your blood sugar. I don't know about you but I get a little dopey and grouchy if I don't eat."

Mitch frowned as he mulled that over. "I have been thinking about the pie from the diner. But I could go for a sandwich or something."

"Special's chicken 'n' dumplings today."

"That sounds good too." Mitch stood and stretched, and Bree took a second to appreciate the way his muscles rippled underneath his shirt. The man was in great shape. For a split second, she wondered what he looked like without a shirt. *Professional, Bree.*

"You okay?" he asked.

"Huh?" Bree shook her head. "Um, yeah. Just thinking."

"Would you like to join me at the diner? I'm guessing you haven't eaten anything this afternoon either?" Mitch asked.

"Oh, okay. Yes, I'll come. Chicken 'n' dumplings sound good to me too." Had she been asked out to lunch by Mitch? Or had she asked him out to lunch? Did it matter or was this a *professional* lunch now that they were actually going to be working together? It was all a little confusing. He held his cards pretty close to the vest, so reading his intentions and emotions was difficult. Maybe he was all business.

Mitch checked in with his supervisor just before they headed out. It sounded like the tactical team would be leaving any moment to try and track down Jimmy Lee.

"SO, CAN YOU tell me what kind of real-life experience you've had in dealing with cults? Or was it just theoretical?" Mitch asked. He had a strong desire to know how well versed Bree was with the subject.

Bree stopped unrolling her silverware and gave him a strange look, then slowly continued placing her knife, fork, and spoon in their correct placement on the table. As she spread her napkin across her lap, she looked up at him again, as if she were deciding whether or not to share something. "I've had…personal experience with one. I didn't realize it was a cult at the time because I was so young, but as an adult, I believe we were lucky to get out when we did."

"Your family was involved with a cult when you were a child?"

"They called themselves a church. My mother was an alcoholic and they took us into their congregation. Momma actually stayed on the premises for six weeks to detox."

"So it was a religious-based group. How long were you members?"

"It's hard to say. Almost a year? Daddy changed during that time. He began treating Momma like she was some kind of terrible sinner—same as the church members did. It was like she had a scarlet letter tattooed on her. They were kind to me and my sister, Darla, and Daddy seemed to like hanging out with the other men. And there was this woman. This horrible woman who was the *worst* to Momma. She seemed especially sweet on Daddy."

"Did they abuse your mother?" Mitch asked.

"They threw her in a dark room with a blanket and a pillow and left her to atone for her sins. She detoxed all right, and I'm guessing it nearly killed her. Once she came home, she wasn't the same. It took years before she was her old self again. Of course, she started drinking again not long after, and Daddy left us for good then."

"You father left his family? Left you to deal with your alcoholic mother alone?"

"He recruited my grandmother to help out, and then we never saw him again after that."

"Is he still alive?" Mitch asked. He was trying to control his rage at the idea of a man leaving behind his young daughters to face the horrors they must've dealt with all alone. "What about your momma?"

"We don't know if Daddy's still alive, but Momma died two years ago. Just before I met Jolene and Jimmy Lee."

"That's what you meant when you said you were going through a lot back then."

Bree nodded.

"I'm sorry." Mitch struggled to find the right words in this kind of situation.

"It's all right. Losing Momma was complicated, emotionally. I was offered the job by the hospital in Moonshine at a pivotal time, so I decided a change might be good for me."

"Was it good for you?" he asked.

"Yes. I think so. I'd broken up with my fiancé around the same time, so getting out of Huntsville was helpful to put that behind me. But I hated leaving my sister. We'd been together our whole lives. It's a challenge—being apart."

"I hope I haven't pried too much." Mitch realized how hard it must be to speak of such difficult things to a stranger.

"No. You haven't. Finding Jolene has kind of brought it all up again, you know? It's been buried at the back of my mind for a long time. My childhood wasn't easy. Momma was never easy, and Daddy's leaving us has been like a little splinter festering all these years. Sometimes I don't even feel it, but it gets sore at other times and hurts pretty bad."

"I understand that kind of pain. My daddy left us, but he stayed around the area. I always wondered if it would've been better if he'd disappeared for good or died. He's continued to cause us pain ever since. He was an alcoholic."

Bree's expression softened. "I'm so sorry, Mitch. People can be so cruel. Even the ones who are supposed to love us the most."

Mitch had to agree with that. "He treated me like I was some kind of freak. Especially when I was diagnosed with autism and Asperger's. It was like he thought he might catch it or something. He was ashamed of me and barely spared me the time of day when I needed him the most. He'd spend hours at the bar around the corner and sit on a stool drinking." Mitch scoffed. "At least we knew where to find him."

Bree shook her head. "I honestly couldn't say which would be worse. The not knowing where Daddy was or knowing, but him being a total waste."

"I guess we really do kind of understand each other, huh? I don't think I've ever met anyone with such a similar story." Mitch felt a kinship toward Bree that allowed him to relax a bit. With her, he didn't have to be on his guard all the time. She understood.

"The key to healing is understanding that our parents' decisions and flaws don't determine the course of our lives.

They cast shadows on us, of course. But we get to choose how to live and to be happy."

"Spoken like a true therapist." He raised his glass of iced tea.

Bree laughed. "We're getting deep for a late lunch. Every therapist has her personal ghosts—I'm convinced. We seek education to help ourselves."

"Makes sense. I appreciate the free therapy. You have a refreshing way of helping me approach my past." Mitch really did feel a little lighter after listening to Bree's perspective.

"Glad if I can help. So, now you know what my cult history is besides my actual studying of it."

"I've got the feeling you are exactly the person we need to help us through this case. Once we get Jimmy Lee back and question him, things should become clearer."

Mitch's phone lit up. He looked at her apologetically and uttered the word, "Calloway."

Chapter Eleven

T HEY'D FOUND JIMMY Lee's truck. Bree and Mitch had returned to the sheriff's office after Mitch had gotten a call from the off-road team. "Let's have a look at the footage from the drone. It's just come in." Mitch and Bree had gone into the conference room with the suits.

It appeared that Jimmy Lee had set himself up a home-built bunker of sorts dug into the side of the mountain. There was a structure, but it was obscured by trees, likely intentionally. This wasn't built by a person without training in outdoor survival. Jimmy Lee had been taught, or he was self-taught in living off-grid. Because the drone could only video the exterior, it was hard to see if there were weapons, or if anybody else was on site. But it was clear that this wasn't a large homesite that housed more than one or two people.

No sign of Jimmy Lee, but he could be inside.

"Looks like Jimmy Lee isn't still with the cult," Mitch said to the group. "I suggest we send the team in to extract him if he's on site."

Special agent Aaron Roberts, Mitch's boss, agreed. "Send them in. Tell them to proceed with caution, as if Jimmy Lee is armed and dangerous, but we want him alive for questioning."

"Yes, sir," the team leader replied and gave the order to his guys in the field. They wore helmet cams, so the video was streamed real time onto multiple screens that had been brought in and were set up for viewing by the suits and agents in the room. There was a lot of shouting of orders as the team burst onto the scene, catching Jimmy Lee completely unaware. He appeared to be skinning an animal under a lean-to around the side of the property and immediately put his hands up and surrendered, dropping the knife he had in one hand.

"We've got him, sir."

Jimmy Lee confirmed that no one else was on the premises, and the agents gave the all clear.

Mitch said, "Tell them to video and photograph everything inside the structure. I want to see how he's been living. How he's set all of this up."

The agent gave the order.

As the video streamed in, Bree noticed neatly lined rows of jars of home-canned fruit and vegetables. There were smoked and dried meats hanging from the ceiling. Jimmy Lee was fully prepared not to starve if he had to hunker down for a long winter. This had taken a lot of work and prep. And knowledge. One didn't just wake up one morning knowing how to can food or smoke and dry meat. He'd learned it someplace. Either growing up in a family who did that sort of thing or while he'd spent time with the cult.

"I'm really impressed by the level of preparedness here," Bree said to Mitch.

"Yes, this is pretty remarkable. It takes years to learn how to do all of this," Mitch agreed.

"Exactly what I was thinking."

Mitch looked over at Bree. "How do you feel about a little trip to the field?"

"I'm in." Bree was fascinated by the idea of seeing how Jimmy Lee lived firsthand.

Mitch said to his boss, "Sir, Bree and I are going to head over to the site and gather evidence. I believe it will be helpful to get a firsthand look at the situation. Afterward, I would like to interview Jimmy Lee."

Special Agent Roberts nodded. "Okay, Mitch. Just be quick about it. I don't want Jimmy Lee stewing too long on ice before we question him."

"Noted, sir. Can we get an escort to the property?"

Roberts nodded and made a call. "There's an off-road vehicle outside with an auxiliary team member we recruited for this assignment as backup. He'll take you over to the site."

"Thanks."

Hannah was at her desk as they were about to head out. She was keeping track of comings and goings for the task force. "Hey, Bree, you want me to take Tiny for you until you get back?"

Bree looked down at her bag where Tiny was happily sleeping. She was torn. Taking him bouncing up a mountain side in an off-road vehicle might be more upsetting than leaving him with Hannah. "O-okay. Are you sure he won't be a problem?"

"No, of course not. Just leave his leash and bag. Do you have a bed for him at your office? I'll get a water bowl from the kitchen."

"Yes, I'll grab his favorite pillow and be right back."

Bree turned to Mitch. "Do you mind?"

"No. He'll be more comfortable here." He reached for Tiny. "I'll hold him while you go and get what you need from your office."

It felt like the most natural thing in the world handing Tiny over to Mitch, which surprised Bree. She was so protective of her little pup. But she knew that taking this job was important and wouldn't be without some sacrifices. Hannah was the most solid and capable person she'd met here in Moonshine. And if anybody would keep Tiny safe, it was Hannah.

She was back in a flash, and Tiny settled quickly on his pillow next to Hannah's desk. He wasn't normally so chill about Bree leaving without him. It was almost as if he was digging deep because she needed him to. Of course, Hannah was already stroking his head, feeding him treats, and telling him what a handsome good boy he was. So, maybe he wasn't having to dig *too* deep.

It took thirty-five minutes to reach Jimmy Lee's little slice of heaven. Twenty of those minutes were spent in teeth-jarring torment bouncing around in the back of the off-road vehicle, clinging to the safety strap just above the window that her momma always called the "Oh Jesus" handle in their car. Bree was infinitely relieved when they arrived and even more relieved that she'd not brought Tiny along for that uncomfortable ride.

"Are you okay?" Mitch asked as he helped her out of the back seat. He'd ridden up front with the driver.

She ran a hand through her messy hair. "I might need a

minute to let my stomach settle."

"Yeah. No kidding. That was intense."

They looked around the area for a few minutes, noting that the camouflage netting strategically hung to disguise the structure was similar to what the military used to hide their operations. "Wow. He really didn't want to be found, did he?" Bree said.

There was a four-wheel all-terrain vehicle under a tarp next to at least a cord of firewood that was neatly stacked next to a large evergreen tree. On one of the larger branches sat a small satellite dish. As they entered the living space, Bree was even more impressed to see it in person. Every square foot was used efficiently. There was no wasted space at all. Jimmy Lee had created a small but comfortable environment with efficiency in mind.

There was a security setup with a two-way radio, a police scanner, and a computer with two monitors that showed trail camera views. Clearly he'd set up cameras in the trees leading up to the property in every direction. The only thing he hadn't allowed for was the police drone they'd used to find him. It hadn't yet been determined if Jimmy Lee owned the land where he'd set up housekeeping. He had clearly been here quite some time. A year maybe? The firewood looked as if it was cured. That took several months at least.

Both Mitch and Bree put on latex gloves so as not to leave any fingerprints behind. This wasn't a crime scene, but it was a place of interest because it was the home of a person of interest. So, they'd have to be careful not to disturb things in case the situation evolved.

Bree made her way through the living space. She noticed

prescription bottles beside the double bed. Mood stabilizer, antidepressant, antianxiety meds, and sleeping pills. So, Jimmy Lee was taking his meds like he'd said. But the name on the bottles was for a Jessie Monroe. The pharmacy name where they'd been filled looked to be a local compounding pharmacy instead of the usual big box pharmacy. He probably paid cash for the drugs and left no trail through insurance. No wonder there'd been no recent medical records. Jessie was likely a nickname or middle name.

"Very esoteric genres here." Mitch was currently looking through some of Jimmy Lee's reading materials.

Bree approached with the meds. "We need to make sure he gets these while he's in custody. Going without them, even for a day or two, could throw him into a bipolar event. Especially since he'll be under stress while he's being questioned against his will."

"Let's bag them." Mitch had brought in his evidence kit. He carefully picked up the bottles and placed them in individual plastic evidence bags and labeled them.

Bree went to have a closer look at Jimmy Lee's nightstand to be sure there weren't any more bottles she'd missed. When she opened the drawer, she noticed a small journal. "Found something," she said to Mitch, who turned and moved toward where she stood holding the book.

When she handed it to him, an envelope dislodged and fell to the floor. "What's this?" Bree bent down and picked it up, noting the writing on the outside of the envelope. "It's Jolene's handwriting." Bree's heartbeat sped up.

MITCH GRABBED THE sheet of paper, carefully unfolded it, and spread it out gently on the bed. He first took a photo of it and then read it as Bree stood beside him.

Dear Jimmy Lee,

I've left the compound and can't return. I'm afraid they'll come after me. Please take care of yourself and stay on your meds. Hoping to see you again once it's safe, but I don't know how or when. I'm scared of your momma and Sarah. As you well know, neither of them would cry at my funeral. I hope you can find a way to get out of there, my love. I can't tell you where I am right now, but maybe we can find a way to be together soon.

Jolene

"Talk about a tragic love story." Bree shook her head. "I wonder how she got the letter to Jimmy Lee inside the compound."

"I wonder how long after she 'disappeared' that she wrote this." Mitch had a lot of questions now. "We need to get forensics in here to search the place from top to bottom to see if there are any other letters from Jolene. Right now, we need to get back and question Jimmy Lee. I've got a feeling he's not going to be a reliable witness, so we'll need as much physical evidence as we can collect to help put the pieces together."

Bree nodded. "I'm beginning to think that Jimmy Lee had motives that nobody knew about in living here and keeping to himself."

Mitch called headquarters and requested a court order for a full sweep of Jimmy Lee's residence both inside and outside. Jimmy Lee wasn't yet accused of a crime, but since this was a homicide investigation and he was considered a person of interest under reasonable suspicion, the law allowed them to search his domicile. He was in possession of evidence that would be useful in helping with the investigation. Plus, he was the spouse of the deceased, with no alibi.

Mitch and Bree hightailed it back to headquarters so they could question Jimmy Lee. Unless they were able to charge him with a crime, they'd need to cut him loose within twenty-four hours. Mitch was hopeful the judge was easily accessible and would sign off on the court order before Jimmy Lee's time on ice expired.

After another bouncy trip down the mountain, they managed to make it back to Moonshine in record time. Bree appeared a little green around the gills, but otherwise seemed fine. Still really pretty as he helped her from the back of the vehicle when they arrived back at the sheriff's office. He did wonder what she was thinking sometimes but hesitated asking. She seemed to have the magical power of looking deep inside Mitch in ways that made him uncomfortable. He wasn't so sure having someone around who actually understood him was a good idea.

They entered the office amid a buzzing hive of activity. Phones were ringing and special agents and law enforcement officers were hard at work. The paperwork during an ongoing investigation was as consuming as the actual investigating. Nothing happened without a requisition and someone signing off on it. Every firearm, Taser, tactical vest, et cetera was accounted for. Plus, there were the laptops, office supplies, and tech. So much tech.

Mitch found his boss first thing. "We're ready to question Jimmy Lee. We found a letter at his house from Jolene and we believe he received it after she'd gone missing. He knows more than he's told us about her disappearance, sir."

The special agent in charge nodded. "He's all yours. Your request for a search warrant is being processed. The judge is considering it now."

"Thank you, sir."

Mitch turned to Bree. "Do you want to come inside while I question Jimmy Lee or would you prefer to watch through the window?"

"I'd like to be with you if that's all right. I won't get in the way. Since he already knows me, it might help. Also, I can see his facial expressions up close. I can tell by his body language if he's telling the truth."

"Okay. Let's go."

They entered the room where Jimmy Lee was anxiously tapping his foot. "What's all this about? How did y'all find me?"

"Calm down, Jimmy Lee. We just need to ask you a few questions." Mitch kept his voice calm, hoping not to get his witness agitated.

"You've got nothing on me and I don't have to tell you anything." Jimmy Lee held his head high and his shoulders back, posture defiant.

"Have you taken your meds today?" Bree asked. Her tone was kind and friendly. "We brought them for you if you need them."

Jimmy Lee refocused his attention on her. His shoulders relaxed just a little. "Uh. No. I haven't. I guess I need to take 'em."

Mitch looked toward the two-way glass and motioned. "Could we get some water and the medication in here?" He'd left the medication with an officer outside of the room, knowing it might be a possibility they'd need them.

After Jimmy Lee had taken his medication, he calmed down a little. Mitch wondered if being away from home and worrying that he hadn't take the meds might have caused some of his anxiety in the first place.

"So, Jimmy Lee, we found a letter from Jolene. It fell out of a book beside your bed when we picked up your medication." Mitch pulled a copy of the letter out for Jimmy Lee to see.

"You went into my house—into my bedroom without a warrant. I'm gonna sue y'all into next year for this." But he stared hard at the letter.

"It was in plain sight, Jimmy Lee. Plus, the warrant is in the works. The more you share with us now, the less we'll need to invade your privacy to find out the answers we're looking to get."

"After Jolene dropped Tiny off, she came back to the compound to be with me. She wasn't happy there and didn't get along with the leader, Sarah, or my mom. Jolene thought they were plotting against her." Jimmy Lee dropped his head to his chest. "I guess they might've been. Momma never did think much of Jolene and wasn't very nice to her. But I told Momma to lay off her."

"How long after she dropped off Tiny did Jolene leave

the compound?"

Jimmy Lee shrugged. "Maybe two weeks."

"How long after that did you receive the letter from her?"

"A couple of days maybe. I kept thinking she would come back, you know? Momma said good riddance and acted like she wanted me to start something up with Sarah."

"Did you have a relationship with her?" Mitch asked.

"I wouldn't call it a relationship exactly. They kind of manipulated me into sleeping with her. She was pretty hot, you know? And she really came on to me after Jolene left. Made me think she was trying to cheer me up."

"Did this happen right after Jolene left?"

"Not right after. But before I got the letter. I felt pretty bad about it later."

"Yeah, I guess so. Your wife goes missing and you sleep with somebody else before you know what happened to her or why she left." Mitch wanted to get a little rise out of Jimmy Lee and see if he would let something slip.

"You don't know how it was for me, so don't judge. And I didn't feel like I could say no. Sarah was...important. She was one of the people in charge at the camp. It was best if you did what they told you, you know?"

"We appreciate your help with this, Jimmy Lee. We want to find out what happened to Jolene, and you are the only person who was with her around the time she disappeared. Can you tell us any more about the Community of Atonement?"

Jimmy Lee's eyes darted back and forth like he was afraid somebody would catch him snitching. "Those are some bad folks, Special Agent. They're still up there in the mountains, and I, for one, don't want them to come down here once they learn that I ratted them out."

"Jimmy Lee, if you give us some solid information right now, I promise you'll have our protection."

Jimmy Lee seemed to weigh that for a moment. He took a deep breath and said in an almost whisper, "They've made a few people disappear, you know?"

"Tell us about that, Jimmy Lee."

"There was a banker from Atlanta. He got tired of the corporate grind and took up with the community. He thought he was taking a nature vacation, you know? Like, all oatmeal and granola and stuff. But when he started making noise about leaving, they told him it would take a little more time to adjust and to be patient."

"What happened?" Mitch asked.

"He agreed to wait. Got all wrapped up in organic compounding and gardening. But after a few weeks, he got impatient again and insisted they let him call his kid. They wouldn't give him his phone back and threw him in a meditation chamber with only a bucket and a couple of bottles of water. No food. I could hear him crying at night. I managed to bring him something to eat when nobody was looking, but that poor guy was a mess."

"What was his name, Jimmy Lee?"

"Bob was all I knew. They take everyone's documents and phones and lock them up when you arrive. I did over-hear Sarah bragging to Momma what a putz he was and how they'd gotten into his bank account through his phone because it wasn't protected with a password."

"So these people steal the members' money and keep them cut off from their families?" Bree gasped beside him. "How did you escape, Jimmy Lee?"

"It wasn't easy. I had to leave at night. Momma is still there, you know. She's taken up with the Master of Atonement. They didn't pay much attention to me because they didn't think I wanted to leave. But once Sarah left on her recruiting trip and she wasn't constantly wanting my attention, I knew my chance had come."

"How long were you there?" Bree asked.

"About six months. I couldn't take it any longer and I missed Jolene. I'd learned how to take care of myself by then. They teach the members a lot of things about living off the grid and how to prepare for it. I learned how to hunt and fish and garden. I thought the canning and pickling stuff was boring, but it came in handy."

"You carved out a pretty nice place for yourself, Jimmy Lee."

Jimmy Lee puffed out his chest with pride. "You bet I did. And I did it for Jolene. But she never came back." He lost his air then. "Do you really think she's dead?"

"I'm sorry, Jimmy Lee. I'm afraid it looks that way."

"Those assholes should pay. I know they killed her. Or they sent one of their people to do it for them."

Bree asked, "Do you think your mother is involved in what's going on up there?"

Jimmy Lee nodded. "I hate it, but I think she's under the master's spell."

"Do you have any idea who this 'master' is?" Mitch asked him.

Jimmy Lee shook his head. "I've seen him a time or two,

but I didn't get a good look. He stays out of sight mostly. He's not always on the property, but anytime he comes, he's in a car with dark windows and they drive him into a garage. Nobody but Momma and Sarah are allowed to go near the big house when he's there. It's not really a big house, but it's the nicest building on the property."

"How many people were part of the community when you were there, Jimmy Lee?"

"About thirty or so, give or take."

"Were most of them happy to be there?" Bree asked.

"Mostly. People who came there didn't do well in the normal world, so getting out of it, for them, was a blessing, I think. Sarah gave lectures on the evils of corporate America, and she worked hard to make the camp nice and friendly for everyone. It was peaceful pretty much all the time, except when people wanted to leave."

"What happens when people want to leave?"

Jimmy Lee shifted in his chair. "I'm pretty sure they were persuaded not to. Kind of like Momma used to punish me when I was a kid and I misbehaved." He stared down at his boots.

"Were they harmed?"

"I came out all right, didn't I?" Jimmy Lee spread his hands out in front of his face for Mitch to see. "Momma knows how to change somebody's mind is all. I'm sure she didn't hurt people or nothing."

Mitch figured he could circle back to that topic later. "Are they still operating in the area?" Mitch asked.

"The last time I heard from Momma, she was tickled about some big businessman from Chattanooga they were shaking down, so yeah, they're still at it."

Chapter Twelve

THEY FED JIMMY Lee dinner at the diner and allowed him to move around the town square with a deputy. He wasn't under arrest, but they needed him for the next steps in the investigation.

Mitch, Bree, and a whole team of agents met with Aaron Roberts, the special agent in charge, to discuss what Jimmy Lee had shared with them.

Bree had been furiously writing notes as she'd gotten information. Now, it was her turn to share her thoughts on a cult profile. She stood, cleared her throat, and began. "According to Jimmy Lee's information, this is a dangerous group of people, I'm afraid. Their motivations are mostly financial but they've created an environment of total control. The leaders are set apart from the rest of the group, creating a godlike power structure. Because of the dire consequences of speaking out against them, their members stay in line, afraid to step out of line. As long as they are willing to go along, things work out well for them."

Mitch said, "The problem we're facing is that we don't have any concrete evidence connecting them to the murder of Jolene Monroe. And right now, all we've got is Jimmy Lee Monroe's statement regarding the crimes the Community of

Atonement have committed. I'm proposing that we infiltrate the community with two undercover agents and get a firsthand look at what's happening inside. We can then learn who the players are and find solid evidence of their crimes."

"Undercover ops are dicey and not our first choice, as you well know, Special Agent. Who do you suggest we send in to the community to do this dangerous work?"

Bree surprised herself by saying, "I believe I should go. With Mitch. I have some inside experience with cult behavior and believe that if we pose as a couple looking for solace from the outside world, we might be believable in this role." Bree hadn't yet discussed this idea with Mitch, but as it formed in her mind, it made perfect sense.

"You're a civilian, Bree. We don't like to send civilians undercover," Aaron Roberts said.

Mitch raised a hand. "Sir, it makes perfect sense. Bree is a seasoned professional in behavioral sciences, so she would know what to look for as we navigate the community. Since we'll be there as a couple, I can stay close and make sure she's safe."

"There's never a guarantee of safety undercover, Special Agent. You know that. Do you know how to use a firearm, Dr. Hawthorne?" Special Agent Roberts asked.

Bree nodded. "I grew up in Alabama, sir. My nana insisted my sister and I knew how to shoot by the time we were twelve or so."

"How long has it been since you've fired a weapon?" he asked.

"Several years," Bree admitted. "I do own a handgun, though."

Roberts appeared to be weighing the pros and cons of this idea. "Mitch, take her out to the range and see if you think she is competent with a sidearm before I agree to this."

"Yes, sir."

"If she's good with a gun, we'll need a phony story. Let's work out a plan to introduce the two of you to the community. You'll need a backstory to plant on the internet." Roberts turned to a woman in a dark suit. "Rosa, can you contact cyber division and get the process started? They'll need to be active on a couple of social media sites. Maybe a space planning background for Bree. Mitch could be a firefighter from Michigan. Just enough so that it's believable. Not too much information that can be checked out."

"Yes, sir." Rosa made a few notes.

Roberts turned back to Mitch and Bree. "Undercover operations aren't my favorite because they endanger my people, but it might be the best way to catch these criminals red-handed and nail them. Cults almost always have a 'burn it down' plan if they get a whiff of law enforcement, so you'll need to document *everything*. We'll fit you both with hidden cameras and wires. They'll take your cell phones the minute you enter the gates most likely. We'll need to stream it in case they catch you."

Roberts turned to Rosa again. "See about getting them some tech that won't be detected. A hat, scarf, jewelry, belt buckle, and the like."

Bree thought about Tiny then and glanced over to where he was happily still hanging out with Hannah at her desk. How could she leave him? He'd think that she'd abandoned him just like Jolene had. She nearly said this aloud, but since going in undercover was her idea, she kept quiet.

Mitch was furiously scribbling in his notebook. "We'll need to sit down again with Jimmy Lee Monroe and get as accurate a layout of the community as possible so we can make a map of the place. We'll need to know where they eat, sleep, gather, garden, and the like. There will be lots of security cameras most likely."

"And let's get a list of as many people on the inside as possible that he remembers too. If people are disappearing, we'll need to know who's been there. Also, we'll need to research missing persons reported from surrounding areas. See if anybody's gone missing after saying they were quitting their job and going off the grid or something similar. Usually, if people tell friends and family, they're taking off, they're not considered missing or in danger, and the case gets filed away."

"Good point, Special Agent," Roberts said.

Bree was fascinated by how thorough Mitch was. His brain was ticking off every scenario one by one. "How can I help?" Bree asked.

He looked up at the sound of her voice and blinked. He'd obviously been so involved in his thoughts that he appeared to have forgotten she was sitting beside him. "You can go and get your gun and any extra ammunition. We have a date at the shooting range at the state police training facility out on Industrial Boulevard in an hour."

"Got it. I'll meet you back here." Bree smiled at him and noticed by his expression that it surprised him. Like something clicked over from working Mitch to man Mitch.

He returned her smile. "See you in an hour."

There was something so refreshing about him, Bree thought. Every time she smiled at him or their fingers brushed, he appeared startled. As if nobody had ever gone out of their way to be kind to him, which caused him to have really low expectations of people—women in particular.

She stopped by Hannah's desk to grab Tiny. "Thanks so much for keeping an eye on him."

"Any time. He's super sweet."

Bree tucked Tiny back into his puppy stroller. She remembered that they'd been on the way to get ice cream when Chase had waylaid them. She looked at her watch. She owed Tiny a pup cone, and there was just enough time to stop by on her way out.

IT TOOK MITCH a few minutes to get back into what he'd been doing after Bree left. The way she smiled at him always threw off his concentration. The woman was stunning and seemed to know just how to get under his skin—in a good way. He frowned, worried now about bringing her into an unsafe situation undercover. Would he be able to ensure her safety as he'd promised?

Nothing was ever certain when it came to undercover operations, especially safety, and they hadn't yet determined how dangerous things were on the inside of the Community of Atonement. He and Jimmy Lee had a lot of talking to do. Setting up an undercover investigation meant planning for every possibility. Knowing what things literally looked like inside was the first step. Mitch relied heavily on mental maps so that he could envision what it would be like moving around the community. They would need to know where the "safe" places were and where the "hot zones" might be. He and Bree would run through all kinds of scenarios and decide what the best course of action might be should things go sideways and they got separated.

He'd never run an operation where he had feelings for someone he was working with. *Do I have feelings for Bree?* It hadn't occurred to him until now. She was attractive. He liked her laugh. He cared about her opinion of him. Was this a good idea? Admittedly, she was smart, had good instincts, and was their most experienced professional on cult behavior on hand at the moment. Mitch didn't work with emotions much. Hadn't ever really. He was a facts kind of guy, so this was confusing for him.

Could they work together without any entanglement? Without attraction or emotion getting in the way of the operation? At this point, there seemed to be no way out of it. His boss was counting on them to do this. Mitch was reliable in his job, and it was extremely important to him to maintain that level of respect, especially since he'd been assigned to lead the investigation.

He made a list of questions for himself and the team. Questions that needed to be addressed before they could create a solid plan for the operation. Many of the questions would be answered by Jimmy Lee hopefully, if he continued to be helpful and honest. The wildcard here was that his momma was part of the cult, and taking them down meant putting her at risk and possibly in jail. If Mitch knew anything it was that it wasn't going to be easy for Jimmy Lee to give her up to law enforcement without trying to figure out a way to keep her safe from harm and from prosecution.

If what he'd said was true, his momma was up to her armpits in trouble, and no amount of finagling and bargaining would keep her out of trouble.

The GBI often went to reasonable lengths to negotiate with whistleblowers, but Mitch doubted they could go so far as to excuse her part in possible kidnapping and conspiracy to commit murder charges, should that be the case here.

Mitch glanced at his watch and saw that it was time to leave to meet up with Bree at the shooting range. The facility was just outside of town headed toward Blue Ridge, so it would take a few minutes to get there. He hoped she was proficient with a firearm. Being scared or unsure when or if the time came to use one could prove deadly. It would also be the determining factor as to whether or not the special agent in charge would allow Bree to participate in this operation.

As he drove to the gun range, Mitch ran through scenarios in his mind for their upcoming assignment. He preferred to envision all likely possibilities so that he could be as prepared as possible. These mental exercises were something he'd always done before heading into any kind of potential combat situation. If he allowed his mind to envision the darkest places—the worst-case scenarios—he could be ready for almost anything that came his way. Right now, though, the worst cases also involved Bree, and they disturbed him like never before.

BREE DIDN'T WANT to bring Tiny to the shooting range because of the noise, so she turned the TV to his favorite show—a silly cartoon that for some reason seemed to soothe him—and left his food and water bowls full. He wasn't a big eater but liked having a full bowl in case he wanted to graze. He shot her a wounded glance as she kissed his head. "I know, buddy, but sometimes I have to go out for a little while."

Bree was intuitive enough to know when it was best for Tiny that she leave him on his own. And honestly, some places just weren't dog-friendly. A gun range was one of those places.

Bree grabbed her revolver and its case from her bedside table and checked the chamber. It was loaded, of course. A woman living alone in a rural area ought to have protection. She unloaded the gun and grabbed the box of bullets from her dresser drawer and dropped another kiss on Tiny's head as she passed through the living room on her way out. "Bye, baby."

Bree remembered finding the gun after Daddy left them. It had been tucked away in a closet out in the garage. When he'd gone, he'd hardly taken anything with him, so this was one more thing she'd had to remember him by. Bree wondered how things might've turned out had he stayed in their lives, even if he'd divorced Momma. Would they have been any better for having him around?

One thing was certain, they'd struggled after he'd taken off. Financially and emotionally. Small children don't understand why their daddies leave. Bree saw it over and over again in her practice, so she knew it wasn't something that was unique to Darla and her. The abandonment left a hole so big they'd never been able to fill it. They'd just worked around it ever since.

Bree would need to tell Darla that she was going to be out of pocket for a week or two and give the GBI Darla's number as her emergency contact should anything happen to Bree. It really hadn't occurred to her until that moment that this could truly put her life at risk. Going into a situation where they didn't know the extent of the danger was a gamble. Oddly, Bree trusted Mitch and his team to help them navigate the situation even though they were having to trust Jimmy Lee as a reliable narrator of the facts.

She was nearing the gun range and saw that Mitch had already arrived as she pulled into the small parking lot. He was standing next to his truck, arms crossed. Waiting for her. Her heart rate kicked up a notch as it always did when she saw him. As she parked, their eyes locked and he smiled. He seemed to be doing that more often when they were together. It was a nice change from the first time they'd met.

Bree reached over and grabbed her gun and ammunition, and it hit her again why they were here. This was serious business. Not a date.

"Hi there," she greeted him as she climbed out.

"Hey." He reached out for her weapon. "Let's see what you've got here." He took the revolver from her. "A .38 caliber Smith and Wesson—a classic. Nice." He looked the gun over, making Bree feel glad that she'd kept the gun clean all these years.

"Is it okay to use? I know lots of people use a newer kind nowadays."

"It's not GBI standard issue but I'd like to see how you handle it."

"Do you think we can get a gun inside the community?"

"I'm not sure how we'll handle that yet. It's another question for Jimmy Lee."

They entered the range, and Mitch showed the attendant his badge, signed some paperwork, grabbed a couple of sets of noise-canceling earmuffs and clear shooting glasses, and they were buzzed back to the range. There was only one other person shooting downrange.

"You ready? Do you need a refresher?" he asked.

"Always point downrange, don't ever put my finger on the trigger until I'm ready to fire, always wear my eye and ear protection, and always unload my weapon between firings."

"That's about it. Let's see how you handle it."

Bree was a little nervous because she knew this was a test and that this test was important to the case. Important to catching a murderer or murderers. She took a deep breath, remembering how Nana had taught them over and over. *Load, stance, aim, breathe, fire.*

Her first shot hit the target's shoulder, the second, the left torso, the third, center torso. She pulled the weapon up and fired again. Two head shots. Bull's-eye.

"Nice shooting." Was that a gleam of pride she saw in Mitch's eye?

"Thanks." She'd passed the test.

He pulled out a gun from his holster. "Let's try this one. It's a little heavier than yours but it's standard issue."

He went through the steps of loading the magazine. "There's one in the chamber, so be aware."

She noticed the weight was significantly more, like he'd said. *Load, stance, aim, breathe, fire.* Her shots were lower this time.

"You'll need to compensate for the weight and the kick-back. The caliber is larger, so aim just a little higher and hold steady." He stood behind her to steady her shoulders.

She shot a few more rounds. Bull's-eye.

"Awesome job, Bree. I guess the op is on." They unloaded the weapon, gathered their guns, and returned the safety equipment.

A wave of excitement followed by panic gripped her as they exited the building. "I'm…a little nervous about this, Mitch."

"You wouldn't be normal if you weren't. If you don't want to do this, tell me now. We can still call it off. You have to be sure, Bree. They'll be able to tell if you're scared."

"I'm scared. But I'm going to be okay. I've just got to work through my nerves. Once we figure out the plan, I'll be fine."

Chapter Thirteen

WHAT BREE LEARNED quickly was that heading into an undercover operation was a full-time, round-the-clock job. She wondered if anyone had slept since they'd greenlit the plan. She'd been allowed to see her patients and introduce them to Jenn, thankfully. That had gone well, and Bree was thrilled that they all agreed to see Jenn next week while she was "on vacation."

Jenn had a calm and engaging way about her that drew people in. Bree was impressed by her manner, and greatly relieved to put her patients in such capable hands—the same with her group therapy patients at the hospital. It was a fantastic way to introduce Jenn to the staff and administration there as well—a perfect way to get her foot in the door while her credentials were being finalized.

Now, she'd need to speak with Sadie about taking care of Tiny while she was out of pocket. Bree decided to stop by her house while she had a minute before heading back into the war room back at the sheriff's office. She knew that once she got back in there, it would be hard to get loose again. She texted Sadie to be sure she wasn't on an important call and had time to see her.

As she approached Sadie and Chase's house, Bree had a

moment of panic. Could she leave Tiny? She parked and knocked at the door. It was lunchtime, and she knew that Sadie took a break from her clients around noon every day.

As Sadie opened the door, she heard Sadie's pup, Daisy Mae, let out a little *woof!* "Hey there. I'm so glad you stopped by. What's going on?" Sadie wasn't one to mince words. She knew something was up. Probably because Bree hadn't ever stopped by her house for no good reason.

She showed Bree in and they sat down at the bar after Bree greeted Daisy Mae properly with lots of pets and telling her what a good girl she was several times. The house was Chase's before Sadie came back to Moonshine. Bree had always loved the house, but she could tell that Sadie had put her stamp on it and made it a little more—feminine. "I'm sorry for the short notice, Sadie. Something's come up. I can't say much except that I'm working with the GBI and the sheriff's department on a case. I've got to be away for several days—maybe a week or even two. I wondered if you would take care of Tiny for me while I'm gone?"

"Of course I will. We love that little guy, and you don't have to worry, Bree. I don't know what's cooking, but I know you wouldn't leave him unless it was important."

Bree teared up then, something that rarely happened. "I hate to leave him, Sadie. I don't want him to think I've abandoned him."

Sadie put a hand on hers. "He will be fine, Bree. I get that you're worried about his emotional state because you and I have both been through a lot, but Tiny isn't going to feel that way with us. Daisy Mae will keep him distracted and playing. I'll make sure he has all the love and chewy bones he wants. I promise you, he's going to be okay."

Sadie had just hit the nail on the head. Bree was definitely projecting her own abandonment by both her mother and her father onto her pup, and Sadie knew it. "I know you're right, Sadie. Thanks for pointing it out."

"Thank you, Sadie. I don't know how much Chase will tell you about all of this, but in case something happens to me—could he stay with you and Chase?"

"Oh, goodness. What on earth is going on? Are you in danger?" Sadie's eyes filled with concern.

"I don't think I will be, but I need to have a plan if things don't go as they should. That's probably about all I should say. Don't worry, okay? They're making sure to do everything possible to keep us safe."

"Now I'm dying to know what's happening. I'll ask Chase though. I don't want you to say anything you shouldn't, and I respect that it's an ongoing investigation. Chase will tell me just enough to satisfy my need to know but also not tell me more than he should. He's good at that."

"Well, I'd better get back. It's busy over there."

"I'm getting the sense from Chase that things are heating up. So far, he's just said it's a GBI case he's helping out with."

Bree nodded. "I'll drop Tiny off first thing in the morning if that's okay. He shouldn't keep you from doing anything. As long as he's with Daisy Mae, he should be fine. He's totally potty trained and is happy in his crate at night."

"Just bring his food and anything you think will make him feel at home here."

Bree left Sadie's house feeling much lighter knowing that

Tiny would be well cared for, and hopefully happy, with his friend, Daisy Mae. She made a mental list of all the things Tiny would need for an extended stay at Sadie's house.

Bree swung by the house and picked up Tiny on her way back to the sheriff's office. There was no reason he couldn't hang out with her or with Hannah until she had to drop him off with Sadie tomorrow.

MITCH HAD A list of questions to ask Jimmy Lee, but he wanted to wait until Bree returned so they could question him together. Jimmy Lee seemed a little more relaxed when she was in the room with them. Just as he glanced down at his watch, Bree came in. "Hi there. I had to speak with Sadie about taking care of Tiny while I'm gone."

"No problem. Are you up for speaking with Jimmy Lee further about his time with the Community of Atonement?"

Bree nodded. "But I was thinking that it might be a more comfortable and productive conversation if Jimmy Lee didn't feel like he were being interrogated like a criminal. What do you think about moving things down to my office where it's quiet, and we could record our conversation?"

Mitch hadn't thought about Jimmy Lee's feelings during all of this as he often didn't. It was one of his blind spots—the feelings of others. Leave it to Bree to consider that they might get more information out of him if he felt comfortable and valued as part of the investigation. "That's a really good suggestion. Let me go run it by the suits." Mitch was lead on this operation, but there was a very well-defined hierarchy in the bureau. Nothing went on without running it up the line of command first.

"I'll wait here."

Mitch made the trip from his small workspace to the conference room in back where the special agent in charge— Roberts—was busy requisitioning paperwork for all of the items they would require during the operation. "How did Bree do at the gun range?" he asked Mitch.

"She's a good shot—got a steady hand. Knows her way around firearms. She shoots with a .38 Smith and Wesson revolver, but I switched her over to a standard-issue Glock and she picked it right up."

"All right, Mitch. Looks like you've got yourself an un- dercover op. We've been moving forward with things under the assumption that Bree would prove adept with a hand- gun."

"Sir, would it be all right if we questioned Jimmy Lee Monroe in Bree's office down the way?" Mitch pointed in the direction of Bree's office. He explained to Roberts Bree's reasoning for the change of venue.

"That's good thinking. Make sure you record the ques- tioning. I'll send someone over now to set up a video camera. We might text you additional questions for Jimmy Lee, so keep your phone on."

"Yes, sir. Where's Jimmy Lee?" Mitch hadn't seen him in a while.

"He's down at the ice cream shop. Getting a little antsy waiting around for us to question him."

"I'll go and find him."

❧

BREE ACCOMPANIED MITCH to the ice cream shop next door. It was almost five o'clock, so she grabbed Tiny from his perch next to Hannah. She didn't want to inconvenience Hannah by making her late leaving, knowing Hannah had a toddler at home. Despite the long hours everyone seemed to be working, Chase insisted that Hannah leave at her normal time. He'd always said she got way more done during the workday than anybody he knew.

Tiny was tucked inside Bree's purse and she hoped that Jimmy Lee's presence wouldn't upset him. The idea that Jimmy Lee might've actually done anything upsetting to Tiny beyond raising his voice was beyond Bree's imagining. It would need to be addressed up front because she wouldn't subject her sweet pup to someone who'd abused him in the past.

"Hey, Jimmy Lee. You ready?" Mitch asked. Jimmy Lee was a scoop deep into a double chocolate chip cone.

"Yeah. Sure. Can you wait until I finish my cone?" he asked.

"Okay. Bree, do you want something while we're waiting?" Mitch asked her.

She shook her head, still thinking about Tiny and patting his little head. She tugged Mitch's arm and he followed her outside of the shop. "Listen, I hate to bother you with this, but I wanted to ask Jimmy Lee if he'd ever hurt Tiny before we got started. If he did, I don't want to subject Tiny to being anywhere near him."

Mitch frowned. "What? You think he actually laid a

hand on Tiny?" Mitch's expression turned fierce.

"I only know that when I met them, Jimmy Lee spoke very harshly to Tiny, telling him to shut up and such when he whined. And Tiny was shaking and nervous the entire time they were in my office. It could've been that Jimmy Lee was having a psychotic break or it could've been that he was abusive toward Tiny."

"There's never an excuse to hurt a defenseless animal or child. Ever." Mitch said this as if he'd seen plenty of both. "How has Tiny been since Jimmy Lee's been back—hearing his voice and all?"

"So far, it hasn't seemed to bother him much. Right now, he's calm and relaxed. I'd be able to feel it if he were antsy or shaking." Bree had been surprised at how calm Tiny was, despite Jimmy Lee's presence.

"Hey there. Are y'all ready to go?" Jimmy Lee stepped outside with the deputy assigned to accompany him.

Mitch's eyes locked on to Jimmy Lee. "Jimmy Lee, did you ever hurt Tiny?"

Jimmy Lee appeared confused. "No. Of course not. I yelled at him some. I was sorry for that cause it was mostly when my head wasn't right, you know."

Bree let out an audible sigh of relief. "Okay. Thanks for being honest. He's with me now and I had to be sure."

"I miss that little guy. We were buddies most of the time."

Mitch pointed down the sidewalk. "All right, let's head on down to Bree's office where we'll be more comfortable. The sheriff's office is noisy and chaotic. It'll be easier to talk where it's quiet."

Jimmy Lee's posture relaxed. "I hate police stations."

"I think most everybody does, Jimmy Lee." Bree was glad that he seemed more at ease with their plan to speak away from all of the hubbub.

She plopped Tiny in his spot and he gave Jimmy Lee the side eye, but nothing more. The camera was set up in the corner and Mitch went through a few disclaimers with Jimmy Lee about recording his statement.

"I'm going to ask you a lot of questions, Jimmy Lee. We need to get a clear picture of exactly what things are like inside the community. I'll need you to help me put together a map of the place from your memory of both the interior rooms and buildings and the exterior to scale."

"I can do that."

"Let's start with you telling me, as accurately as possible, how many people you can remember who were there when you left, and who they were. Also, who might've gone missing—either run away or in some other way—while you were there."

Jimmy Lee frowned. "I don't want to get Momma in trouble."

"What has she done, Jimmy Lee?"

"I'm not exactly sure if she's done anything illegal really. I just know how mad she's gonna be at me if I rat her out to the police and turn everybody in. I know it'll help us figure out what happened to Jolene, but you don't want to see Momma get mad. She's pretty fierce if you know what I mean."

"We don't know what you mean, Jimmy Lee." Mitch stopped for a moment.

"Jimmy Lee, if your momma was abusive to you growing up, I understand why you might still be intimidated by her now. But you know she can't hurt you anymore, right?" Bree interjected because this was her area of expertise and she knew childhood trauma when she saw it, and Jimmy Lee was filled with it right now.

"She didn't exactly beat me or anything. But she'd get mad and teach me lessons—leave me by myself for a good while in the dark. I didn't like the dark. I'd get hungry and she'd tell me that hunger was God's way of teaching us hard but beautiful lessons. It didn't feel beautiful, I gotta tell you."

"It sounds like she was tough on you, Jimmy Lee. I'm sorry about that. Did you leave the community to get away from her?" Mitch asked.

"Momma took care of me when I had my first mental break, and if it wasn't for her I don't know what I'd have done. Jolene and I were together by then and she didn't know what to do, so she let Momma take the lead on that. After we got my brain chemicals back on track, it was like Momma didn't want me to get too far out of her sight, you know? Jolene and Momma weren't the best of friends after that. Jolene thought Momma was controlling and overbearing, and she wanted for us to live our lives without Momma right there in the middle of us."

"Makes sense. Do you think your momma had something to do with Jolene's disappearance?" Mitch asked.

Jimmy Lee shook his head. "Momma wouldn't have hurt Jolene because she knew that I loved her. For all that Momma was tough, she did love me. I left because I thought if Jolene came back, we could be together, and I knew she would only come back if I wasn't still inside the community."

"How did you get out?" Mitch asked.

"I had to lie and make a break for it. I couldn't let Momma know I was planning to leave for good because she'd have never allowed it. She was too worried about me relapsing with my bipolar disorder. I had to take what I'd learned inside the community and put it to good use on my own. Built a nice place for Jolene and me. I just wish she'd have come back to me."

"So your momma never found you after you left? The two of you aren't in contact anymore?" Mitch was busy making notes as Jimmy Lee answered.

Jimmy Lee shook his head. "Never saw or spoke to her again after I left. I didn't go too far from the community either. They taught me well how to blend in with my surroundings and disappear into the landscape."

"Who owns the land where your place is, Jimmy Lee?"

He snorted a laugh. "That's the thing. It's owned by the community as far as I know. It's about twenty miles away on the roads, but they showed me a map one time of all of the land they'd bought up in the area. Lot closer as the crow flies through the mountains."

"Who is they?" Mitch asked.

"The Master of Atonement. We just call him Master. Don't know his real name. He stays in the shadows. Won't have his picture taken. Wears a hat all the time. Hard to even say what he really looks like. Momma knows because she took up with him just as soon as we go to the community. If you ask me, she knew him from before."

"Before what, Jimmy Lee?" Mitch asked.

"Before we got there. It seemed like they were old friends—or maybe acquaintances. I'd never met him as far as I knew. But maybe I did when I was a little kid. We'd gone around to some of those kind of weird churches back then."

That gave Bree pause. "What do you mean, 'weird churches'?"

"You know, where they'd speak in tongues and stuff. They got all carried away during their praise sessions and their eyes would roll back in their heads. Felt really intense. Momma always liked to go places like that. We'd hang around for a while at one church and then move on to the next one. Daddy really didn't get into it much, so the two of us stayed home a lot while Momma spent her time at church."

"What happened to your daddy, Jimmy Lee?" Bree asked.

He was quiet for a few seconds. "He up and died one day. Choked on a piece of meat at dinner. Momma had left his dinner warm in the oven that night and took me to a church meeting with her. When we got home, we found him there on the kitchen floor." Jimmy Lee shook his head. "I'll never forget seeing him like that."

"I'll bet. Sorry you had to witness that." Bree grimaced at the idea of little Jimmy Lee seeing his daddy dead on the floor with a piece of meat stuck in his throat. "How did your momma react to finding him deceased?" she asked.

"She was upset. Tried to revive him, I think. But he was gone. I was just a little kid and I could tell there wasn't no coming back from that."

"What happened after that?" Bree wanted to get a clear picture of what Jimmy Lee had gone through as a child at the hands of his cult-loving momma.

"We stopped going to church for a few years. Momma got a regular job at the phone company to pay the bills. I could tell that she tried to be like the other moms mostly, but she still taught me the hard lessons when I acted up. We lived in our same house but I wasn't allowed to have friends over until I met Jolene in high school, and after we graduated, I had my mental break. Things went kind of haywire after that."

"When did your momma start back going to church?" Mitch asked.

"When I was in junior high, I think. By then, I didn't have to go with her, so I really wasn't sure where she went or who she spent her time with outside of work. By the eighth grade, I was smoking weed after school behind the gym most afternoons. Self-medicating, I've been told."

Bree nodded. "Most likely."

They'd been sitting and talking for almost three hours when Mitch got a call from the special agent in charge insisting they take a break for the evening with Jimmy Lee. "We're to start again in the morning, Jimmy Lee. You should go get something to eat. The GBI is putting you up in the B&B down the way."

Jimmy Lee nodded. "Well, I guess that's all right. How much longer do y'all think we'll need to talk before you try to bust the master and his followers?"

"Not sure yet. I know you want your momma kept out of this, but it sounds like she might be in it pretty deep,

Jimmy Lee." Mitch sounded sympathetic to Bree's ears, which was a good thing. Sometimes Mitch got involved in just the facts because of his inclination to be so analytical. It was a trait that was common in those with left-brain tendencies, and also those on the autism spectrum. The more she observed Mitch, the more she realized that he'd worked very hard to find balance despite his different cognitive and social abilities. It was impressive.

"Yeah. I been thinking about that. I don't really know what she has or hasn't done, honestly. I hope she didn't hurt anybody, but I know she can be harsh sometimes. And she likes to please the master."

"You're sure you don't know his name?" Bree asked.

"Nope. No idea."

"What about Sarah? Could she be his daughter?" Mitch asked.

"I really don't know. She was there when me and Jolene got there, and Momma acted like she liked Sarah better than Jolene, which made Jolene really mad."

"That had to be really hard on Jolene. I don't blame her for being upset with the situation," Bree said.

Jimmy Lee squirmed in his seat. "Y'all said we were stopping now, right?"

Mitch nodded. "We'll see you bright and early here in the morning at eight o'clock."

"Roger that." Jimmy Lee gave a fake salute to Mitch. "Gonna go to that diner and grab a couple of those peanut butter and banana sandwiches. Kind of gotten addicted to them."

Mitch turned off the recording equipment and Bree

locked up the office.

The deputy joined Jimmy Lee and headed toward the diner, while Bree and Mitch headed back to the sheriff's office. "What do you have planned for dinner this evening?" Bree asked.

"Nothing planned. Gonna take a quick break and get back to work. You?"

"We could eat together if you want."

He smiled. "I would like that."

Chapter Fourteen

TINY HAD BEEN a sweet boy, sleeping off and on during the interview, so Bree took him outside to potty as soon as they were all done and then tucked him in his carry bag. She suggested they head over to the Italian restaurant on the other side of the ice cream shop for a change of pace. Plus, neither of them wanted Jimmy Lee to think they were following him around.

"It smells so good in here." Mitch inhaled the scent of garlic and possibly yeast rolls. "I hadn't realized how hungry I am."

"They have the best shrimp scampi here. And people love the clams—if you like clams." The hostess seated them at a small table in the back corner.

"I love clams." He opened the menu and looked over at Bree. She'd worked hard right alongside him today. "We make a good team, don't we?"

She nodded. "I think so. I was impressed at how you questioned Jimmy Lee without making him feel uncomfortable. I get the impression he and his momma were really close despite the fact that she's pretty much a monster."

"Yeah. I guess you can never underestimate the bond between a boy and his momma. Especially when there's no father around. I can relate to that for sure. My momma was a good person and wouldn't ever have done what Jimmy Lee's did, but I can imagine what he went through having only her as a parent until he met Jolene. And then to lose Jolene like that. He must be in real pain." Mitch spoke as he perused the back of the menu.

"It's curious though how he cut his momma off in hopes that Jolene would come back to him. I feel like there's something he's not telling us."

The server arrived with glasses of water. Mitch ordered a Diet Coke and Bree a ginger ale. "Could we go ahead and put our order in now? We're a little rushed." Mitch hated to hurry, but he felt the need to get back to work. He ordered the clams and Bree got the shrimp scampi over a bed of angel hair. "Why do you think something's off with Jimmy Lee's story?"

She took a sip of water. "He cut his momma off permanently and built a house out in the woods hoping Jolene would come back to him? Surely he had a more solid plan than that. They must've been in contact beyond what he told us."

"Hmm. You're probably right. But when did they lose contact?" Mitch had to agree with Bree there. Something wasn't quite right. "If he won't tell us the truth, it's up to the evidence to tell us."

Their food arrived in record time, and they spent the next ten minutes filling up on fabulous garlicky pasta and seafood. The rolls were to die for. "They're gonna hate me at the station with all of this garlic. Good thing my desk isn't too close to anyone."

Bree laughed. "I know what you mean. But it's so worth it."

"Are you headed home after this?" Mitch asked.

"Yes. Unless you need me tonight."

"Not tonight. Spend some time with Tiny. I know he's going to stay with your friend tomorrow."

Bree's eyes got a little sad. "Yes. It's hard for me to part with him even for a few days. I feel so responsible for his happiness." She reached into the satchel beside her and petted the pup.

"I understand how you must feel that way after Jolene leaving him with you. Must've been hard on the little guy."

"Yes. He's been a little clingy ever since." Bree wiped her mouth with her napkin. "So, I was wondering where you were staying while you're in town."

"I'm at the B&B down the block, same as Jimmy Lee. The other special agents are spread out at the local rentals and two hotels near the lake, so we can come and go at all hours." The B&B had six rooms, and three of them were currently booked by the GBI.

"Y'all are lucky to have gotten rooms at peak season."

"We've got a little pull. Any cancelations went to us instead of the next person on the list. Fortunately for the owners, we pay really well for our accommodations."

After they'd eaten and Mitch paid the bill with his GBI credit card, they strolled back to Bree's office. She'd pulled Tiny out of his cozy confinement and Mitch carried him like a football, tucked between his bicep and his forearm. The pup was completely relaxed against his side. Mitch felt a little guilty asking Bree to part ways with Tiny, even for a few days. "I hope you know how much we appreciate that you've offered to help us with this case. I know it's a sacrifice."

Bree looked up at him, as if she were surprised. "Thanks, Mitch. That's kind of you to say."

"I know I sometimes forget to say the right things, but I do understand how people feel for the most part."

She nodded. "I know you do. You've been great with Jimmy Lee."

"Thanks. I try to remember to stop and think about how he must be feeling after losing Jolene and how hard it must be for him to be estranged from his momma, despite their odd relationship."

"Yes, I'd say it's odd. They were probably co-dependent his whole life until he met Jolene. I'll bet his momma didn't take it well when he found someone to replace her."

"No, probably not. That reminds me, I need to call my mother before we go dark. She'll wonder where I am."

"I'm glad you're still close with her. I miss mine so much, despite our difficult relationship throughout my life. The booze was her Achilles' heel. I often wonder what kind of life we all would've had without her addiction. I wonder if Daddy would've stayed."

Mitch could hear the familiar longing in her voice. It perfectly matched the same longing he'd always known.

"Yeah. I understand the wondering how things might've been. I sometimes wonder if my dad might've not hit the bottle if I'd been more of a normal kid instead of—well—instead of like I was. Like I am." He could hear the sadness in his voice. Sharing feelings and personal stories wasn't something he'd done with anyone—ever.

They stopped in front of Bree's office and she took his free hand. "Mitch, there's absolutely nothing wrong with you. You're a kind and caring person. You're smart and intuitive, and sensitive. Just because some diagnosis back when you were a kid said you were different in some ways doesn't mean you have to wear an invisible sign around your neck with a label. What's made you different has made you the perfectly unique individual that you are, Mitch Calloway. I wouldn't want to know you any other way."

Mitch felt an unfamiliar lump gather in his throat and he coughed a little to clear it. "Thank you, Bree. That's probably the nicest thing anybody beside my mom's ever said to me." He smiled at her to break the tension of his deep sadness. Bree was right. He *had* borne his diagnosis like everyone could see it—like a flashing neon sign. But he believed her words. Nobody could see it. They didn't know he was on the spectrum just from meeting him or working with him.

Everybody had differences, didn't they? He could point to almost everybody he knew and see at least one glaring oddity about them. Some people laughed too loud and too often, others were rude and grouchy, and one special agent he knew picked at his fingernails incessantly.

"You're one of the more 'normal' people I've met, and I don't mean compared to my patients." She laughed, and he laughed. And again he worried about bringing her into a cult where they had no way of guaranteeing her safety. He was beginning to like Bree Hawthorne more every day. If something happened to her on his watch, he wouldn't be able to live with himself.

AFTER SHE LEFT the restaurant and got home with Tiny, Bree decided to take a long, hot bath and call Darla. They hadn't talked in several days and she needed to tell her sister that there was a chance she would be out of pocket for a little while. It might be the last time Bree would be able to have an evening at home to relax for quite some time in the foreseeable future too.

Darla answered on the first ring. "Hey there, Bree." The sound of her sister's voice always made Bree smile.

"Hey, girl. How's it going in Alabama?"

"Oh, you know. The same as always. Trying to juggle the job and stay sane. I'm home now though. How's it going in Georgia by the lake?" Darla loved Bree's little house on the lake and tried to visit whenever she could.

"Well, it's getting a little complicated at the moment, which is why I wanted to call you."

"Complicated? As in, you've gotten yourself involved in another kidnapping case? Or, complicated, as in, you've met a dashing man and you're running away to see the world?" Darla referred to the last big case Bree had profiled with law enforcement, and it *had* been complicated and quite a dramatic couple of months. Certainly not the dashing man part—well, not really that.

"Something similar to the kidnapping case. It's a murder case this time. I'm helping with that. I'll need to go out of town for several days and I'm not sure when I'll get back, so I wanted to let you know in case you tried to get in touch and couldn't."

"Since when would you be completely out of touch? We communicated before even when you were in the thick of things."

"True. But this will be a little different. Where I'm going is out in a mountainous area without much cell service. It will be very spotty, so I wanted to prepare you just in case." Bree had no intention of telling her only living relative that she was possibly putting herself at risk, and that there was no way to get in touch while doing so.

"I don't like the sound of that, Bree. It's hard to imagine a place where I couldn't reach you if I needed to." Bree could hear the twinge of anxiety in her sister's voice. They'd always been close, a closeness born out of necessity and love. And sometimes desperation, due to their parents' behaviors throughout their childhoods. Mostly Momma's, but after Daddy left, both girls had felt alone in a way that only orphaned children could relate to. It was a shared experience that was unique to them as sisters. A bond that nobody else understood.

"I'll make sure you have an emergency contact number in case you need to get in touch." Bree tried to keep her voice light, but she doubted she could fool Darla.

"I hope that whatever this super-secret thing is that you've gotten yourself involved with is a smart idea, Bree. You know I worry about you, right?"

"I'll be fine, honey. I feel compelled to help with this, and I'm kind of uniquely qualified for this particular situation, so I'm needed." All of which was true.

"You have a servant's heart, that's for sure. If it had been up to me, I don't know that Momma would've made it as long as she did. You had so much patience with her and her drinking. So many times I was ready to give up on her." Bree could feel Darla's admiration.

"I was older. It was my job to make sure Momma was taken care of."

Darla scoffed. "It was Nana's job, really, but she'd already thrown her hands up years before you took the reins. At least she took care of us while you took care of Momma. Too bad Daddy threw in the towel so early on."

"Daddy wasn't the man we thought he was, and there's nothing we can do to change that." That bitter disappointment was still hard to swallow after all this time.

"No, you're right. I don't know why I keep bringing it up." Somehow so many of their conversations ended up with one or the other of them pondering why Daddy left or where he was. Or so many other unanswered questions they still had about their mysterious father.

"Probably because it's our biggest unsolved mystery in our lives. Maybe deep down, if we could figure it out, then maybe everything else would make better sense. Like a missing puzzle piece, you know?" That was the best Bree could do for wisdom tonight.

"Ooh, that's a new one, Bree, and a good one. I'm impressed. All this police work is making you really sharp. Any new cute cops?" Darla asked.

"Um, there is this one guy. He's really different, but we're not involved like that." Were they?

"Hmm. Sounds intriguing. Tell me more."

"My water's getting cold and I've got to feed Tiny. He's going to stay with my friend, Sadie, and her dog, Daisy Mae, tomorrow for a few days while we go up in the mountains."

Darla was quiet for a minute. "You're not bringing Tiny?"

"Uh, no. I've been asked not to." Better to blame administration than admit it might not be safe.

"I'm just a little surprised. He's never been away from you since you got him. This must be a really intense situation you're heading into."

"No, it's just that I don't know what my schedule will be like—" true enough "—and it's not really dog-friendly."

"O-okay. I'll let you go and feed Tiny. Please call me when you get the chance so I don't worry, please."

"I promise that I will as soon as possible. Love you, Darla."

"I love you too, sis. Please take care."

As they hung up, guilt weighed on Bree. She hated lying to Darla.

She climbed out of her now-tepid bath and dried off, wrapping herself in her soft, terry robe. Tiny hated anything to do with bathtime and remained on his bed situated under the towel rack in the corner of the bathroom. Bree got the feeling he knew something was up, so she pulled out one of his favorite chewy bones as a treat. More guilt gnawed at her over her impending abandonment of Tiny.

Guilt rated at the top of her least favorite emotions list. For someone who tried very hard her entire life to do what was right so she didn't feel guilty, Bree was experiencing a lot of that particular emotion right now. Trying to do what was right had currently landed her here, unfortunately.

When she was a kid, Momma would beg for booze, and

Bree wouldn't get her any or wouldn't tell her where Daddy or Nana had hidden it if she did know where it was. Momma would throw tantrums, and she would cry for Bree to help her. Bree felt horrible guilt for not helping Momma even though she knew she was doing the right thing regardless if Momma threatened her and Darla with terrible consequences if they didn't do what she wanted. So Bree struggled her entire childhood and young adulthood, feeling guilty about something or another. After Momma died, she thought maybe it would get better. But she realized that there was always something to feel guilty about. And right now, she was feeling a double dose of it.

Bree poured a glass of wine and cuddled with Tiny while they watched a sweet and funny rom-com that never failed to make Bree smile despite whatever was happening around her. It was interesting how the hero in the film reminded her a little of Mitch. She would return to her guilt tomorrow.

MITCH APPRECIATED THAT he'd gotten a room within walking distance to the sheriff's office. The place was nice and the owner was a salty little lady with purplish-gray hair who cackled when she laughed.

This was a nice town and the residents he'd met so far were all welcoming and cordial. Of course, he'd gotten a couple of sideways looks when they got a glimpse of his badge, or maybe it was that he was wearing "church clothes" in these parts. Either way, there was a warmth to the town and a charm that was undeniable. And then there was Bree—

certainly another mark in the favor of Moonshine.

Mitch sat down at the desk in his room and made a list of all of the people Jimmy Lee had mentioned while they'd spoken to him today. Tomorrow, they'd need to get a much more specific list of names. People who might've come from out of town and been members of the community. Those who lived and worked within the community that Jimmy Lee might not have known well. They needed an accounting of who was there while Jimmy Lee had been inside. Because if they were gone, where did they go? The possibilities were numerous, and the number of potential witnesses countless. How many family members had missing loved ones who'd found their way to the North Georgia Mountain Retreat looking for a place of peace and escape from the wear and tear of the chaotic world? Those folks, who'd instead tangled with the Community of Atonement and their thieving, kidnapping, and possibly murdering cult.

The GBI currently had agents researching missing persons from the Atlanta and surrounding areas whose family members called law enforcement with concerns that their loved ones had intentionally left their jobs and homes, but then had gone missing after that. Those who weren't actually considered missing to law enforcement. Mitch couldn't imagine how angry he'd be if someone he loved wound up kidnapped or murdered after being blown off by police after filing a report, only to learn that a tragedy could've been prevented if only someone would've taken a closer look at the situation.

He thought about Bree as a young child and how her family had gotten mixed up with a church cult, and how she'd never forgotten it. Now, she was determined to help bring down this group who was harming others, possibly families like hers. He appreciated that she had an inside knowledge of how they worked, but he wasn't sure bringing her back into that kind of environment was the best thing for Bree, though she'd assured him she bore no real PTSD from the experience—only strange and unsettling memories.

Mitch was fascinated by Bree's upbringing and impressed with what a strong person she was, growing up and caring for her alcoholic mother and looking out for her younger sister even after their father had left the family. He'd believed his childhood to be tough, but she might have him beat.

He admired her and her willingness to put others' needs ahead of her own. Now, she would do it again by leaving Tiny with a friend and heading into an unknown situation, a possibly dangerous one, to help solve a murder and maybe save others who might be held against their will.

Chapter Fifteen

B REE DROPPED TINY off with Sadie and Daisy Mae at eight o'clock the next morning. All of the anxiety and worry evaporated as soon as Tiny saw his friend, Daisy Mae. The two pups went tearing off into Sadie's very dog-friendly backyard and did major zoomies round and round until they both rolled onto their backs next to a giant bowl after having lapped up what seemed like a gallon of water. "They're going to have a blast together, aren't they?" Bree grinned and wondered if this wasn't exactly what Tiny needed. A fun vacation with his pal.

"He'll be fine here." Sadie laid a hand on Bree's shoulder.

"I know. I've been so focused on abandoning him that I didn't see what fun this could be for him. Maybe it's me who has the problem." Bree almost laughed when she spoke the words as she helped others realize this very thing so often in therapy. People regularly thought their issues were caused by others, but when they sat down and really studied things, the realization struck that indeed their behavior, thought patterns, and habits were the cause of their woes. "I've just had an 'aha' moment."

Sadie laughed. "Those are kind of nice every now and then. So, promise you'll at least not worry quite so much about Tiny's emotional well-being while you're saving the world, okay?"

"Deal."

Bree left Sadie's house feeling lighter than she had since learning she would need to leave Tiny. Now she could focus on her upcoming role in the investigation with Mitch. She would be lying if she denied experiencing a tingle of excitement, despite the danger. Bree was no adrenaline junkie, but this whole undercover operation had gotten her heart pumping like nothing had in quite some time.

Maybe it was the mystery or that they were walking into the unknown, but it was *interesting*. Mitch was interesting.

Bree had no idea when they would be leaving to join the Community of Atonement, but it must be any day now. She knew the tactical teams were busy preparing for every possibility to ensure Mitch and Bree's safe extraction when necessary and maintaining a perimeter surrounding the compound close enough to get to them quickly when the time came. The team also had to stay far enough away not to alert the community's security cameras or trip alarms.

She'd packed up a small suitcase and duffel with a week's worth of casual clothing items and toiletries. She assumed that nothing fancy would be required at a nature retreat, but she did throw a T-shirt dress and a pair of flat sandals in just in case. It sounded silly to plan her clothing packing for a cult, but she hated not being prepared for anything. Must be her Southern upbringing.

For today, she wore business casual attire, which was slightly less dressy than when she was seeing patients because she knew that it would be another long day and Bree chose comfort over style—yet still appropriate for a work day. Likely, she'd be dressed more casually than Mitch in her wide-leg linen pants and V-neck cotton tee and white tennis shoes. Mitch almost always wore at least well-pressed dress pants, a dress shirt, and tie.

Before, she hadn't thought much about what she'd worn. Her clothes were just something she threw on every day. But she had a new awareness that Mitch was watching her, noticing her. She didn't get the feeling that he was judging or anything, but she wanted to be appropriate. Qualified. She wanted his respect as a professional. Yes, she was overthinking. Maybe it was because he'd initially been skeptical of her qualifications. Mostly, it was because he was so good at his job and she respected him so much.

She entered the sheriff's office at eight thirty, and as usual, it was a hive of activity. Phones were ringing and people were shuffling to and fro. But today seemed a little extra frenetic. Bree looked over at Hannah, who as usual, wore her headset and was talking into it while typing. She looked up to catch Bree's curious gaze and motioned her over.

"What's going on?" Bree asked.

"Jimmy Lee is back there with Mitch already. He wanted to tell Mitch some things he remembered first thing this morning. Got here around seven o'clock ready to talk. Mitch said to send you in as soon as you arrived."

Bree frowned, wondering why Mitch hadn't contacted her already. "Thanks, Hannah."

She hustled to the two-way mirror where she could see Jimmy Lee and Mitch in deep conversation.

"Good morning, Bree," Special Agent in Charge Aaron

Roberts spoke from the corner of the viewing area. She hadn't even noticed him sitting there.

"Oh, hi. Good morning. I feel like I'm late."

"Nah. Settle in. Best not to interrupt this at the moment. Jimmy Lee has decided to go all in with us and divulge everything he knows. I'm not sure why, but I think he's done some thinking about his momma and concluded that she's likely done some pretty bad things."

"Is there anything more about Jolene?"

"He's mainly told us more about how they would recruit people into the community and cherry-pick those who had money and very little family to come looking for them. They apparently have some ties in the city."

"So it's a network?" Bree didn't like the sound of that at all.

"Not a huge one, but enough so that they've lured several disgruntled folks up to the mountains and fleeced them for all they had."

"And then what?" Bree was terrified to hear the answer.

"Sometimes they just shamed them for their stupidity enough so that they'd never admit it to anyone that they'd been taken in like that. Or, sometimes, according to Jimmy Lee, they'd threaten a loved one or two to keep the victim silent. Tell them that they knew everything about their family and would hunt them down if word got out."

"Typical terror tactics. Shame and fear. Disgusting." Bree couldn't hide her contempt for the way these people had ruined the lives of others. "Have they actually murdered anyone?"

"Jimmy Lee isn't sure. Says a few have gone missing besides Jolene."

She could hear Mitch asking Jimmy Lee to write down every person he'd ever met in the community and where they'd come from, what their role was while they were there, and if they'd left while he'd been present. Apparently everybody was assigned a job within the community. Some were gardeners, some did laundry, some cooked. There was always a driver to take Sarah and Glynnis—Jimmy Lee's mother—out of the compound for errands.

Bree's phone lit up. *Are you here?* It was a text from Mitch. He was texting her while Jimmy Lee was busy writing.

Just outside.

Mitch motioned to her to come inside. Bree looked over at Agent Roberts to be sure he was okay with it.

"Go on in. Looks like they're at a good stopping point."

Bree let herself inside the interrogation room. "Good morning. Sorry I'm running late. I had to drop Tiny off at a friend's house." She tried not to allow herself to feel miffed over Mitch not immediately contacting her to let her know that Jimmy Lee was there early and ready to spill his guts on the community's activities like he hadn't been before. Since they'd been acting as a team, it hadn't felt right to her. But he was running this investigation, so she didn't really have a say in the matter.

"Mornin'." Jimmy Lee nodded toward her.

"Good morning, Bree. I hope all went well with Tiny this morning." Mitch sounded sincere, so she felt bad for her momentary irritation with him. She knew that he had a soft spot for Tiny and he knew how anxious she'd been about leaving him, so it made sense that he'd given her some time and space to handle his drop-off this morning.

"Yes, he's very happy to be with his friend, Daisy Mae."

"Jolene did the right thing leaving him with you, Bree, but I know she missed that little guy. They didn't allow pets in the community. Something about people being too dependent on animals and other things for false happiness. Plus, they didn't want to deal with the noise and the mess. That's what Momma said, anyway."

"That's a shame. Did you have a pet growing up, Jimmy Lee?" Bree asked, swallowing the lump of sadness at the idea of Jolene missing Tiny.

Jimmy Lee shook his head. "Nope. Never did. Noise and mess, just like Momma said."

"Sounds like she made some of those rules in the community. Do you know how long she was there before you and Jolene joined up?" Mitch was back to making notes.

"Gosh, I honestly don't know. I hadn't lived with her for a long time and she didn't really talk about her comings and goings, you know? I knew she kinda went from church to church over the years, but didn't know where she'd ended up once me and Jolene got together."

"Why do you think she moved around so often?" Bree didn't like the sound of that.

Jimmy Lee scratched his head. "I don't think any of them ended up liking her much. She was uh, kind of mean sometimes. Told them things they didn't like to hear."

"Like what?" Mitch's pen paused.

"She says they were always too soft on their sinners. Told them how they should stop talking so much about forgiveness and more about damnation and hellfire."

Mitch and Bree shared a look. "I guess that didn't go over too well in most places of worship."

"You'd be surprised how some of them took to it for a time before they told Momma to take a hike. Especially for their hard cases."

A chill ran through Bree, remembering what they'd done to her momma. "I'm not too surprised. What did you say your momma's name was?"

"Glynnis Monroe." Didn't ring a bell with Bree.

MITCH AND BREE took a break in speaking with Jimmy Lee at lunchtime. One of the agents had brought in box lunches from a sandwich shop on their way over from the GBI offices in Calhoun. It helped to have lunch brought in so that nobody had to leave the office and break away from the work they were doing.

Mitch knew he needed to have a conversation with Bree that he dreaded, so he waited until they'd both finished their lunch. "Hey, Bree, I need to discuss something with you."

"Oh, okay. What's up?" He took in her long, blonde hair and light blue eyes.

"How do you feel about changing your hair color?"

She reached a hand up instinctively and touched her head. "Um, I've never thought about it. I've been a blonde since I was a child. I mean, I get highlights now, but who doesn't?"

"I mean, we need to change your hair color for the case.

We always alter our appearance when we go undercover, especially when an agent has such a strong identifying characteristic like your hair."

"Oh. Well, hair tends to grow out, I guess. It won't be permanent."

"Have you ever worn contacts?"

"No. My vision is good."

"You'll need to get fitted for some brown ones. Those blue eyes are memorable." He hated trying to change anything about her.

"Goodness, I had no idea."

"I know, and I'm sorry. We can't take the chance that anyone will recognize you. It's unlikely, but always possible."

"What are you going to do to change your appearance?" Her eyes twinkled as she asked the question.

"You'll see. This isn't my first rodeo." He grinned at her. "I hope you like blond guys who wear contacts."

"No *way*. Seriously? That'll be an interesting transformation."

"You can have your stylist do your hair if you'd like. It might be easier," Mitch offered.

Bree smiled. "Merilee will love this. She's always up for a challenge. Of course, I won't tell her why I'm doing it."

He was relieved that she seemed to accept this as a challenge and didn't seem too upset by it all. "We're getting close now, so you might want to schedule with her in the next day or so."

"That soon?" Bree's eyebrows went up.

Mitch nodded. "We're going to start the scripts today."

"What are the scripts?"

"Our stories. Separate and together. Life history. We'll need to learn it and memorize it all so if either of us is asked a question about ourselves or each other, we can answer without any hesitation. We're going in as a married couple. Once we get the information, we might be more comfortable at your house, if you'd like. How about we pick up dinner and sit outside on your deck? It works best if we're relaxed. Something about how our brains retain information better when we're not trying to cram it in while stressed."

Bree nodded. "I'm familiar with that research. I work with young people who have test anxiety. I suggest the same thing while preparing for exams and class presentations. Taking extra time helps as well."

Mitch nodded. "I wish we had extra time to do it right. Unfortunately, the boss is concerned that people are in danger given what Jimmy Lee has come forward with. He's moving up the timetable to ASAP."

"I can see why he would want to do that."

"This morning, before you came in, Jimmy Lee drew a rudimentary map of the Community of Atonement's grounds and buildings. He described what each structure's purpose was and who could usually be found there while he lived there."

"I'm assuming that was very helpful to give us a picture of what we can expect things to look like."

"Yes. Very." He began to show Bree the different areas of the compound, where the mess hall was, the sleeping quarters, the gardens, and the gathering hall, et cetera.

"I can almost picture it."

"It's the missing piece that we needed for the team to be

able to set up a perimeter. Jimmy Lee also gave us a pretty good idea of where the cameras are and how often things are patrolled since he worked security while he was there. There are a couple of blind spots we can exploit. But we don't know exactly how much security there will be because we don't know how much things have changed since Jimmy Lee was there. There are so many variables."

"I hope he's as reliable as he seems."

"So do I. Unfortunately, he's our only lead, so not trusting him isn't an option. The tactical team has been given the layout and is memorizing what we believe the scale of the compound is. So, they'll be doing tactical rehearsals to get ready for positioning their people around the perimeter."

"I guess everybody has to know their role, huh?"

"To the letter. Since we're uncertain what we're dealing with, it's going to be fluid from the time we get inside. The cameras inside the tech props will help them get a better idea of how they need to support us. It will be up to us to be convincing and not give ourselves away."

Mitch glanced at his watch. "Time to round up Jimmy Lee. I want to ask him more about how he's evaded his momma since leaving the community. Seems odd that they haven't found him after all this time."

Chapter Sixteen

J IMMY LEE DIDN'T seem to have a good explanation as to why the members of the community hadn't found him since he'd left the confines of the compound. Maybe his momma hadn't wanted to make an example of him like she knew she'd have to for leaving should they find him. Maybe they had found him and were keeping tabs on him. If that were the case, then they were all in a heap of trouble. Bree understood this was a calculated risk the GBI was taking.

Either way, law enforcement would have to move in and infiltrate the compound due to the many concerns raised by Jimmy Lee and because they'd found the remains of a member who'd fled their confines. In the end, the GBI had probable cause to search and investigate the Community of Atonement. They were working on getting a warrant ready for a judge to sign should things go sideways. But it would be much better if they could ease in and find solid evidence before the cult lawyered up and fought them tooth and nail. So, the plan stood, and Bree and Mitch were scheduled to go undercover the next day.

Later tonight, however, they would run through their scripts and prepare their stories so that when they did go inside, they would be as believable as possible in their roles as husband and wife. After the transformation, she would head over to the optician at the Walmart to get her brand-new brown contact lenses.

"Girl, I have no idea what kind of bee you've gotten in your bonnet to do this, but I've gotta say, this is my Super Bowl, and I *love* it!" Merilee's eyes sparkled as she grinned at Bree.

"It's time for a change, you know? I've had my hair the same my whole life." Bree kind of meant that but was a little terrified too.

"I wish more folks came in here and put their hair in my hands like that. This is gonna be *epic*, girl."

Bree had to believe that Merilee knew of what she spoke since she was the most popular hair stylist in town. Merilee had slid her into her schedule after her lunchtime today when Bree had explained what she'd needed and that it was a veritable emergency. "I can't thank you enough. I'm headed out of town tomorrow and I just *had* to get this done before I left once I'd made up my mind to do it." Bree hated lying to her friend, but it had been an emergency.

"Where's little Tiny?" Merilee asked as she began to rinse the color off of Bree's hair at the shampoo bowl.

Bree tried to relax as the warm water flowed over her scalp. All of this lying wasn't good for her soul. "He's hanging out with Sadie and Daisy Mae while I go out of town."

"Gosh, I've never known you to leave him with anybody. I hope you're going someplace fun." Merilee wasn't exactly nosy—she was direct. Bree had always appreciated that quality about her until this moment.

"It's actually a quick trip for work. Unfortunately, no pets allowed."

"Ah, gotcha. Well, I know that Sadie and Daisy Mae will take great care of him while you're away."

"Yes, he's in good hands."

Bree checked her phone as the color processed under the dryer. No messages from Sadie about Tiny. So far, so good, she guessed.

Merilee asked, "Are you ready for a haircut?" She wrapped a warm towel around Bree's head and led her back to her styling chair.

Bree could feel the butterflies in her belly despite her agreeing to the makeover. This was getting real. "I-I think so."

"How about a shoulder-length shaggy bob?"

"Sounds good."

"Maybe you shouldn't look until I'm finished." Merilee bit her lip as she unwound the towel from Bree's head.

"That's probably a good idea."

Merilee grabbed her scissors and went to work. She clipped up the top layer of Bree's hair and began cutting length from the bottom. Bree watched as long pieces of sizzling auburn hair fell to the floor all around her. Her hair. *Holy smokes!* What had she agreed to?

She tried not give in to the urge to bolt from the salon. Bree knew rationally that it was only hair, but emotionally, it was part of her identity and had been her whole life. She was a big-haired blonde from Alabama. But not anymore. Becoming someone else for this role was far more unnerving than she'd believed it would be.

Bree kept telling herself that this was only temporary. It was an exercise in patience and anxiety while Merilee finished her haircut.

"Are you all right?" Merilee asked.

"Um, sure."

"Just checking. Your breathing sounds more like Tiny panting under that cape."

"I'm okay. A little nervous, maybe."

"Well, I'm done. Let me get you dried and styled." She fired up the blow dryer and the curling iron and in what seemed like five minutes she was done.

"Are you ready?" Merilee asked.

Bree took a deep breath, willing her heart rate to calm as Merilee spun her chair around toward the mirror.

She didn't realize her eyes were closed until Merilee laughed and said, "You can open your eyes now." Bree did and almost didn't recognize the woman in the mirror.

"Wow."

"You are stunning. I mean, you've always been stunning, but that color really sets off your features."

Bree stared at her reflection. She had to agree. The auburn color was rich and warm and pulled out the deeper tones in her skin and brows. Her blue eyes really popped. "I love it, Merilee."

"I hardly recognize you."

Bree didn't tell her that that was the point and Mitch's goal was achieved. "Thanks so much for squeezing me in."

"Don't mention it."

Bree paid Merilee, slid on her sunglasses, and scooted out the door to her car. Now for contact lenses.

MITCH WAS EATING a second sandwich and a bag of chips when a woman approached his desk. "Can I help you?" He barely glanced up from where he'd been looking over the scripts they'd handed him a few minutes ago.

The woman cleared her throat and he looked at her, his eyes widening. "Bree? Holy cow, is that you?"

"You said to make a change."

He couldn't stop staring at her as a redhead with amber eyes. "It's—striking. I mean, really *hot*." It's the only word that could truly describe the change.

She laughed. "Maybe I should have done this years ago."

"You'll have to give me a few minutes to get used to the change."

"I'm not used to these contact lenses yet. I've never had them before."

"What kind did you get?"

"The monthly ones. I have to take them out and put them in solution every night."

"I know it's a pain but it really changes the way you look."

Bree nodded. "It does."

"I've got our scripts if you want to head home. I can pick up dinner on my way out to your house."

"What's your plan for food?" she asked.

"I haven't really made one yet," he admitted.

"How about I stop by the store and pick up stuff for dinner and you meet me at my house in an hour?"

"You sure?" He didn't want to overstep. It had been his

idea to impose on her at her home for dinner tonight. But they needed to go over the scripts together, so it made sense.

"Of course."

"All right. I need to speak with my boss for a minute and then I'll wrap up."

"Do you have any food allergies or preferences?" she asked.

Mitch shook his head. "I'm pretty easy to please. Not allergic to anything."

"Great. See you in a bit."

"Walk in here and let the boss see you first."

"Oh. Okay." She followed him into the conference room where Aaron Roberts was standing over a large-scaled map of the Community of Atonement's compound that was spread out over the conference table that ran the length of the room. There were lots of notes and arrows already written on the map showing tactical planning.

Special Agent Roberts looked up for a second and nodded at Mitch, and all but ignoring Bree standing just to Mitch's side as if she were invisible, showing that he had no idea who she was. "We're going to head over to Bree's house to go over our scripts where it's quiet, sir."

Roberts raised his eyes again and then comprehension dawned in his eyes. "Bree?"

Bree grinned. "Pretty good, huh?"

"I'll say. I didn't recognize you." Roberts continued to stare at Bree as if he were looking for a hint of her old self. "Remind me to use your stylist the next time we need someone."

"Yes, I thought you'd be impressed. So, we're gonna

head out now." Mitch pointed to the door with his thumb.

"Yeah, yeah. I'll expect you back here at seven in the morning. We'll get you both suited up with tech and have a run through with tactical."

"We'll be here first thing. Night."

Roberts held up his finger. "Oh, and travel light. Don't bring anything identifying. We'll supply you with everything you need besides clothes and toiletries. And don't get fancy with those."

"Yes, sir." Bree and Mitch answered at the same time.

They headed outside together. "You might as well grab your overnight bag and plan to stay at my place tonight. I'm sure we'll be up late going over things. You'll probably get more sleep in my guest room and we can ride in together in the morning if that works for you. We can stop by the store on our way to my house and pick up something to eat."

Mitch nodded. "Okay. That makes sense. I'll just go and grab my stuff. Where are you parked?"

"Just in front of my office over there." She pointed toward where her little red Audi crossover was parked.

Mitch couldn't get over Bree's transformation with red hair and brown eyes. He was sure that her own sister wouldn't recognize her like that. She was beautiful both ways, but it relieved him to know that nobody could identify her in that disguise. Because where they would be wasn't so far geographically from where they were now, the odds were higher that they might run into somebody one or the other of them might recognize or who might recognize them.

Usually, the undercover ops only lasted for a few days—sometimes only a few hours depending on what kind of evidence they needed to ensure their case would be airtight. A successful sting often required someone admitting to doing something illegal additional to evidence already gathered. It might mean getting something damning or someone naming an accomplice or perpetrator on an audio recording, or recording a video of a crime being committed before an arrest could be made. Mostly it was the icing on the evidentiary cake.

Mitch would grab some hair bleach at the grocery store for his disguise. He had his contacts with him since they'd been in his office drawer at work. The last time he'd been there he managed to slip them into his briefcase on the off chance he might need to go undercover. One never knew with this job. Bleaching his hair and putting in a pair of contacts wasn't so hard. But it made a huge difference in his appearance. Almost as much as Bree's new look.

As Bree sat in her car and waited for Mitch to join her, she quickly called Sadie to check on Tiny. According to Sadie, Daisy Mae had kept Tiny so busy chasing him around her backyard that Tiny was completely pooped and barely finished his dinner before dropping onto his bed and falling deeply asleep. That was one thing Bree could mark off her list of worries. She then texted Jennifer to find out how her day went with Bree's patients. Jennifer had no complaints, so Bree mentally marked that one off her list as well. She looked up from her phone to see Mitch approaching with a duffel in one hand and a pair of shoes in the other.

Bree almost laughed. Of course he wouldn't put shoes in the bag with his clothes. She wasn't quite sure of his reasoning, but it likely had to do with shoes being dirty or them wrinkling his clothes. Funny how well she'd gotten to know him in such a short amount of time.

She unlocked the car doors and he slipped his duffel on the back seat, careful to place the shoes on the floor mat. "Thanks for waiting."

"Are you packed for our time away?" Bree asked, noticing that his bag wasn't big enough for more than overnight.

He nodded. "That's what took a few extra minutes. I'd already started preparing, but I wanted to have everything ready for tomorrow so I could swing by and grab my bag before we leave."

"I've got my things ready too. I did that last night."

Bree drove out of the downtown area and stopped at the local market. It was a nice grocery store that also had a good selection of organic and whole foods. Their prepared foods selection was extensive, and Bree often stopped in to pick up dinner on her way home.

"Wow, this is really nice. If I lived in town I'd probably eat here every day."

"It comes in handy as a single person for sure. It feels wasteful to cook a full meal for one person." Bree enjoyed good food, but preparing meals alone wasn't much fun.

"I know what you mean." Bree could hear the underlying loneliness in his voice and identified with it. No matter how fulfilled a person might be in their career and social life, it was lonely to come home to an empty house every night. To face eating meals and watching TV with nobody to talk to.

After selecting salads and then entrées from the hot section, they perused the aisles together, stopping in the wine section and choosing a bottle of red. Mitch paid for their items with the GBI credit card.

"Even the wine?" Bree asked.

"It's part of the meal, and no, we're not breaking any rules."

Bree believed him because she knew him to be a rule follower, same as her. "Okay. Good."

"You know the lines can get a little blurred when we go undercover, right? Things aren't quite as cut and dried as we'd often like them to be." Mitch must've picked up on her hesitation.

"In what way?" Bree asked, wondering what kind of lines he was referring to.

"Well, the entire time we're in there, we'll be lying. For people like us, lying is like breaking rules. It goes against our nature, so we naturally resist it. Try not to let it get under your skin. Instead, try to think of what we're doing like performing a role in a play. It's your job to pretend and do it very well. Well enough to catch the bad guys."

"Mmm, that's an interesting way to rationalize behavior. I usually advise against going against one's true nature, but I guess this might be why my conscience has been tweaked a little. Because I don't know what I'll be forced to say or do to pull off this role."

"My point exactly." They checked out after Mitch grabbed a box of Miss Clairol hair bleach.

Once they'd gotten back to Bree's house, she immediately caught herself as she was about to call Tiny. She missed her little buddy so much already.

Mitch carried his duffel, shoes and had a couple of grocery sacks hanging from his fingers. "Where do you want things?"

Bree pointed toward the kitchen. "Groceries there, and you can put your things in the spare bedroom down the hall. Second door on the right. The bathroom adjoins."

"Thanks."

She carried in the other two bags and uncorked the wine to let it breathe. Bree had chosen a honey chicken entrée with sweet potatoes that looked good, and Mitch got the pot roast and mashed potatoes. He was so different than many of the men she'd known in some ways, but also appeared to be a meat and potatoes guy. She'd bet his mom made a mean pot roast on Sundays. Often people made comfort food choices based on emotion and a connection to a memory.

She began heating her food in the microwave and was reaching for wineglasses when Mitch entered the kitchen. "Do you need some help?"

"No. I'm just getting things warmed up. You can either use the microwave for yours or do it on the top of the stove."

"I'll just wait until you're done. No point in dirtying dishes."

She offered him a glass, and their fingers brushed as he took it from her. His were warm with callouses, and she got a momentary whiff of his aftershave, as she often did working so closely with him, but they rarely had any physical contact. Bree thought physical contact with him might be really nice.

Their eyes locked as the handoff was made. His gaze reflected her thoughts. "I hope we get the chance to spend some time together after this is over."

It sounded a little absurd since they'd been together every day for the last couple of weeks. And they were going into an undercover situation together. "Isn't that what we've been doing?"

He shook his head. "Not what I meant."

Bree knew what he meant, and she broke the eye connection. "I'd like that."

They carried their food and the wine outside once it was ready and sat at the table staring out at the lake. It was dark, but Bree had strung some outdoor lights along the back of the house that provided just enough light to see what they were eating and each other. She'd never thought about this being a romantic setting, but that was the vibe currently between them.

Once they'd finished their food, Mitch stood, cleared their plates, and said, "I'll go and get our printed scripts from my bag."

That hadn't been romantic, but Bree understood that getting involved with Mitch romantically at this moment was a bad idea. They both needed to focus on the job at hand. But after…

He returned and handed her a multi-page, printed and stapled stack of paper. "We are Michael and Jessica Lawson. From now until we head out tomorrow, we should call each other by our aliases."

"Michael and Jessica. Okay."

Chapter Seventeen

M ITCH AND BREE were to be Michael and Jessica Lawson. They'd met at a bar in Atlanta just after Christmas six years ago. Michael was a firefighter in town from Michigan visiting a friend in Buckhead, and Jessica was job hunting after finishing an online course in office space planning. Michael liked the warmer weather and Jessica so much, he moved to the Atlanta suburbs to be with her. Mitch filled Bree in with more background details and they practiced their spiel. Apparently, it was important not to offer anyone specifics unless asked, so nobody ran to fact-check on the internet.

They ran through scenarios of conversations that might occur when meeting others once they were inside the community. Mitch and Bree were able to ad-lib their own stories by creating the names of mutual friends, where they'd lived most recently, siblings, parents, and shared experiences. It helped to make their story feel authentic if they came up with it together.

At some point in the evening, they went inside and continued their discussion in the living room, sitting close together, laughing, and bonding as a pretend couple. Mitch reminded her that they would need to occasionally touch during conversation, or they wouldn't pull off being a believable married couple. So, he gently took her hand while they continued, helping them both to get familiar with the touching. Bree understood that casual and intimate touch likely didn't come easy for Mitch. Sensory issues were often part of even the mildest form of autism and Asperger's.

Touching Mitch, even casually, had a profound effect on Bree, and she wondered if he felt the same now that they'd gotten past the initial moments. She suddenly felt more alive, and it added a dimension to their interactions that hadn't been there previously. It was so much more—personal. Skin-to-skin touch, even just hands, changed everything. It had been a long time since she'd touched a man, and she'd missed it.

"I think we'll be able to fake our way through this as long as we don't say anything specific if anyone questions us separately. Stay as close to the original story as possible." Mitch stretched and yawned, his shirt tightening on his shoulders. He had no idea how attractive he was, Bree was sure of it.

"I guess we should turn in. And it might be the last good night of sleep we get for the next few days." Bree knew that she had a hard time sleeping anywhere but her own house and bed, so it was going to be difficult no matter where else she was.

"Yes, it will be an adjustment for us both."

Bree realized then that they would be expected to sleep in the same room—in the same bed since Michael and Jessica were a married couple. The thought of sleeping that close to Mitch caused her a ridiculous little thrill before she could stifle it with common sense. They were both adults, of course, but there was a real risk in getting too attached and too attracted, maybe for both of them.

Bree had been thinking about Mitch even when they weren't together working. He'd really gotten under her skin, and the thought of this case ending and not seeing him again caused her real distress. She couldn't go there mentally right now since they hadn't even gotten started with the real undertaking yet. What they were doing was important, and looking beyond it wasn't good for the kind of focus this sort of situation required.

Bree said good night and went into her bedroom to get ready for bed. She washed her face, brushed her teeth, and changed into her pajamas, and could hear Mitch in the other room doing the same. What would happen when they were sharing the same bathroom and doing those things together? It would be so…intimate. And she wondered how "off-grid" the place would be. Would it be like camping, like really roughing it? She wasn't accustomed to that kind of discomfort in her living situation. But she would do her best to accept the circumstances, as she understood she'd signed on for the job. Still, she had to admit, it gave her pause.

Bree tried to go to bed, but almost an hour later, her nerves were beginning to get the better of her, so she double-checked that she hadn't forgotten anything she planned to take with her tomorrow. She curbed the urge to text Sadie and check on Tiny, knowing it was too late at night. Had she locked the patio door after they'd come inside? Better check.

As she tiptoed out of her bedroom, she nearly plowed

into Mitch leaving his. She put her hands out to keep from falling as she hit his rock-hard bare chest, and his arms instinctively grabbed her upper arms to steady her. Bree notice his blond hair then. "Gosh, I wouldn't recognize you."

"Yeah, I hardly recognize myself for a day or two. I was just going to make sure the door was locked." He wore a pair of long cotton pajama pants, thankfully. If he'd only been in boxers, she might've lost her cool. The bare chest had set her heart thumping. It was really something.

Bree laughed. "Great minds, huh?" She separated from him and moved ahead down the hallway and headed toward the door, which she'd locked, apparently. "Do you want a bottle of water?"

"Sure."

She grabbed one for each of them from the fridge, trying to avoid staring at his torso.

"Are you nervous about tomorrow?" he asked.

She nodded.

"That's perfectly normal, but we should try and get some sleep."

Easy for him to say. She wasn't half naked.

MITCH HADN'T SLEPT well, probably because he'd dreamed about Bree all night. Worrisome stuff, likely due to some underlying worries about heading into this operation half blind and worrying if they could pull it off. The tactical team had sent up a drone early this morning, so they should have some better intel by the time he and Bree arrived at the office.

"Good morning." Bree looked a little sleepy too. She was brewing a pot of coffee in the kitchen when he walked in. "Coffee's almost ready." She had two to-go cups with lids sitting beside the coffee maker. By now, they'd shared many cups of coffee over the past couple of weeks, so she knew how he liked his and vice versa. She was wearing denim shorts with a white T-shirt as she'd been instructed to by the team. He couldn't argue with that. Those legs of hers were...unexpected.

"Thanks." Mitch tore his eyes away from her legs and saw that her bag was sitting by the front door along with her purse, and he set his beside it. He appreciated that she was efficient and organized. "Anything you want to go back over this morning?" He referred to their scripts.

Bree shook her head. "I'm as ready as I'm going to be, I think." She handed him his coffee and they headed out the front door. She locked up behind them but paused a second and stared at the house before turning and moving toward her car, where they loaded their things.

"Everything okay?" He hoped she wasn't getting cold feet.

"Yep."

They drove in silence to town and Bree parked her car behind the sheriff's office as Chase had instructed her to do so nobody would ask questions about her car sitting out front for days on end.

"You two ready for this?" Chase was there waiting for them, as was Randy Slade.

They both nodded and were ushered to the conference room for briefing. The tech people showed them their accessories first. "It looks like something from a James Bond movie." Bree's eyes were wide as she took everything in. There was a simple necklace with a tiny stone that was actually a camera with an audio device. Both had a pair of sunglasses that had video capabilities. For Bree, there was a small hair clip that she could use even with her shorter hairstyle that had audio. Mitch's belt buckle had a camera, and Bree's purse had a listening device embedded inside the lining, so even if she wasn't in the room, wherever the purse was, it could record conversation.

"I had no idea y'all would be able to see and hear everything we were doing." Bree sounded a little relieved.

"We'll be with you every step of the way," one of the technicians assured her.

"You know your scripts?" Special Agent Roberts asked them.

"Yes, sir. We're ready," Mitch answered for them both.

"Here are your comms. Obviously don't talk back if you can't, but we'll be in your ears feeding you information as we learn anything you might need to know. You do the same." Roberts handed them two very small earpieces that were invisible once in place.

"Did the drone catch anything?" Mitch asked.

"They've got the footage ready now." Roberts pointed toward one of the screens. He nodded to the tech, and the screen lit up. It was kind of dark but could be made out. The compound appeared well laid out with several buildings. The tech paused the video. "You can see that the smaller structures look to be cabins where the members bunk. There appear to be two or three separate quarters to a structure. The larger structure here appears to be a community hall or central meeting place." The tech pointed these out on the screen. "Then, over here must be the mess hall. You can see the dumpsters out back."

"Yes, this checks out with the map that Jimmy Lee drew us." Mitch also noticed the gardens and the parking area, and the watch tower. "Is this the 'master's' quarters over here?"

"Looks like it. It's separate from the others." Just like Jimmy Lee had said.

The drone pulled back and they could see the surrounding terrain then. "We've identified cameras with infrared here, here, and here. Looks like if we set up outside of this perimeter, we should be undetected." The tech circled a large area on the screen using the laser pointer.

"What about the roads?" Mitch asked. "Won't there be cameras at the entrances to all of the roads leading to the compound?"

"The team will hike from the foothills instead of using the roads. They're already headed that way. It was better to have them go out in the dark."

"When are we leaving?"

"As soon as we confirm your cover story as to why you're seeking out the community and how you knew about them."

"How did we find them?" Bree asked.

Roberts pulled something up on his phone. "On a website called 'One With the Earth.' The online team has turned up a few reports of folks chatting online about the group in a forum there. There's a link to the Community of Atonement on the site. It's vague but invites those who are disillusioned with corporate greed and our capitalistic society. Oh, and mention how our food is poisoned and that fossil fuels are killing the earth."

The tech nodded and added, "Yes, any or all of those buzz words will go over well with this group. Sound a little desperate, and you'll fit right in."

"Got it. We can fine-tune the story on the way over. Bree, as a corporate space planner, you've witnessed the very worst of human nature. As a former firefighter, I've seen too much death by toxic chemicals from pretty much everything killing people before the fire even touches them. We're sick of the greed and the focus on artificial happiness."

"That sounds about right. It's not too far from the truth, really." Bree nodded and shrugged her shoulders.

"Okay, I'm checking in with our tactical team. Let's check your luggage and make sure you're not carrying in anything that will get you in trouble." Two agents pulled everything from their bags and laid it all out on the large conference table.

Mitch noticed Bree stiffen.

BREE FELT VIOLATED when her underwear was rifled through a pair at a time. Then her bras, and her toothbrush. She had no secrets, but it still felt like a defiling. She was a private person, and this was awful. She looked over at Mitch.

His eyes told her that he was sorry about this. But she

knew it was for both of their safety. Still didn't make it feel any better.

"Here are your phones. We've taken the liberty to do some pretty good photoshopping of the two of you together using your alias hair and eye color from some old photos. Since neither of you like social media much, we created a Facebook account for your business only, Bree, in Jessica's name."

"How did you do that so quickly?" Bree asked.

"You'd be surprised what the latest AI software can do." The tech showed Bree the photos.

"I can't believe it. It looks like we've been together for ages, looking like we both do now." Shocking really, how natural they looked together—and how strange they both appeared with their odd hair and eyes.

After their bags had been repacked, phones loaded with bogus contact lists, photos, and calendars, they did some last-minute wardrobe shifting, with Bree adding the camera hair clip and pendant to her outfit, and Mitch switching out his belt for the tech one, which looked a lot like the one he'd had on. It was strange seeing him in faded jeans and a T-shirt instead of his usual dress pants and button-down. Casual was equally sexy on him.

Bree was also dressed casually in denim shorts and a white T-shirt with silver hoop earrings. She wore a pair of white sneakers with low-cut socks. Their attire had been suggested by the team to be casual and comfortable. No designer brands. Nothing that would cause the community to pre-judge them in any way.

Finally, they were on their way with Mitch driving a red

pickup truck she'd not seen before. "Whose truck is this?"

"I'm not sure, really. But if I had to guess, the plates are registered to one Michael Lawson."

"Of course they are." Nothing would surprise Bree at this point. The ability of the GBI to invent people, their lives, and photos out of thin air was nothing short of amazing. And the many ways they had to surveil Mitch and Bree while they were inside the compound made Bree feel like the entire team was right beside them. And yes, she did feel better about doing this knowing she had that kind of backup.

But nerves were kicking in now that they were alone finally and heading toward what they both knew to be a dangerous cult. The team was in place, according to the intel they'd just received. So far, so good. Bree thought about Tiny and how much she missed him. She wondered when she would see him again and if he was worried that she'd abandoned him.

Mitch turned left onto a second dirt road that had a small sign with an arrow that read, *Community of Atonement 1 mile.* The tech people had found the community online and gotten the address off a message board, but it had taken some serious digging to find it. People heading to the Community of Atonement had been seriously disillusioned with everyday life and were searching for something very distanced from a nine-to-five existence. As Jimmy Lee had said, quoting his momma: "Those folks are asking for it."

The terrain was uphill and very bumpy, but the road was well traveled, so it was nothing like getting to Jimmy Lee's place. When they finally arrived, there was no doubt because of the plain signage and a large gate barring the entrance to the compound.

There was a man in a small booth at the entrance who stepped out as soon as he saw them approach. "Can I help y'all?"

Mitch stopped the truck, pasted a big grin on his face, and slipped into character, surprising Bree at how natural he sounded. "Hey there, friend. We're looking for the Community of Atonement. We found y'all on the internet, and it says you'd welcome us with open arms."

"Is someone expecting you?" The young man appeared suspicious, his brows drawing together.

"Were we supposed to tell somebody we were coming? I didn't see that, did you, honey?" Mitch looked over at Bree.

Bree smiled back at Mitch. "No, I didn't. We're so excited to finally get here. Got our bags packed and everything. We left it all behind us—our jobs, our families, everything—to come out here and get back to the way things were meant to be."

"Hang on a second." The security guard stepped back inside his booth and spoke into a walkie-talkie. They couldn't hear what he said, but a second later he stepped back out and said, "Y'all gotta leave your phones here before you go in."

"Will we get them back?" Bree asked as she made a point to read his nametag. "Jeff?"

"Cell phone use is limited here in the community. You'll learn more inside." Jeff pointed as he opened the gate. Mitch handed him their phones.

"We're just so glad to finally be here. We don't need our phones. Got nobody to call do we, sweetie?"

Bree smiled at Mitch. "We only need each other."

Chapter Eighteen

THEY'D BEEN BROUGHT to the center of the community, where a woman met them. "Welcome to the Community of Atonement. My name is Blythe." Bree recognized the woman immediately. She was older of course, but she had the same eyes. One was blue and the other brown. It was the same woman from her childhood—the one who'd been so horrible to Momma at church when she'd sobered up that time. Her name wasn't Blythe either. This was Jimmy Lee's Momma, Glynnis.

Bree forced herself to smile, though, despite her shock. Someplace in the back of her mind, she'd wondered if she'd come face-to-face with this evil again. There was no way that "Blythe" would recognize her. She'd been ten years old when they'd last met. "It's so nice to meet you, Blythe. We're just pleased as punch to be here, aren't we, honey?" She laid it on thick and grabbed Mitch's hand.

He squeezed hers back. "Boy, isn't that the truth. While we were trying to get things wrapped up and ready to leave, we talked and talked about how great it would be once we finally got here. This place is awesome." They looked around the courtyard, where admittedly, things were well kept and attractive. There were pots of geraniums overflowing with

blooms, a large grassy area with benches to sit, and a foun-
tain in the center. A sidewalk surrounded the central park-
like area. It was hot, but there was a breeze up in the mountains that the city never had in the heat of a Georgia
summer.

As they talked, a few bystanders gathered to watch. Bree
noticed that they were simply dressed but clean. No makeup
or jewelry. She tried to ascertain from their expressions if
they were anxious or afraid. Curious maybe? Hesitant to
make eye contact? Bree smiled at a woman who was nearest
to her. "Hi, I'm Jessica."

The woman's gaze darted toward Blythe in question.
Blythe nodded. "I'm Destiny. Welcome." She smiled at Bree
and then excused herself and walked away. It was important
they get as many names and faces recorded as possible.

The others seemed to get the hint and suddenly had
someplace else to be as well, because they disappeared as
quickly as they'd shown up. "You arrived just in time for
lunch. The others have already eaten but the food is still out
for the kitchen staff. I'm interested to hear more about what
brought the two of you here." Blythe indicated they should
follow her. They made their way to what Bree knew was the
dining hall from Jimmy Lee's rudimentary map and the
drone footage. She was surprised at how comfortable the
space was once they were inside. She looked up and down
and turned all the way around so the team could see the
entire room through her pendant.

The walls were done with shiplap painted a pale blue.
There were skylights on the ceiling, and around fifteen tables
that seated six to eight arranged in the center. There were

paintings and other artwork on the walls. Maybe done by the members? The food smelled good, and Bree realized that despite the stress, the coffee and protein bar from this morning were long gone, and she was hungry. "This is nice."

She hadn't forgotten for one moment, however, that she was in the company of the same woman who'd thrown her mother in a filthy cell with only a bucket to relieve herself in as she detoxed for days. And she thought about Jimmy Lee's stories of her neglect and abuse. Blythe wasn't to be trifled with, and Bree understood that despite their backup team, they were on her turf now. The goal was to gather evidence and put these horrible people in jail, not blow her cover ten minutes into the operation.

"Is it not what you expected to find up here in the mountains?" Blythe asked.

"Oh, no. It's just a nice surprise. We weren't exactly sure what to expect. There weren't a lot of pictures online. We searched and searched for the right place, you know? We felt called here. Everything we read pointed here as our destiny."

"Yes, we feel lucky to have found this community," Mitch said. They sounded like a couple of the same mind who'd found what they'd been seeking.

"We've got some rules here you'll need to learn. Not everybody is a good fit to live the way we do out here. It's a different life from what most people are used to. First, we don't allow contact with the outside world for a few weeks. This is to help new members acclimate to our enclosed society. There's no coming and going. We earn our privileges here. You will learn to grow food, spin yarn from sheep's wool, hunt, tan hides, smoke meat, pickle and preserve fruits and vegetables. This is a way of life. If you don't think you are up to the task, it's better that you leave now." Blythe stared at them both as if she were measuring their worth.

"We aren't afraid of hard work, are we babe?" Mitch asked. "We came here to learn how to live without television and electronics. Like people used to live back in the old days."

Bree nodded. "Like the pioneers. We read books about that kind of stuff."

Blythe visibly relaxed a little. "Well, we're not exactly pioneers, but it's a lot like that. Hard work and not a lot of frills here. We eat what we grow and kill. And we save and preserve for the coming year because in this world, you never know what tomorrow will bring. Corporate greed is killing the environment."

Mitch and Bree nodded enthusiastically. "We say that all the time."

"No leaving trash anywhere at any time. Always clean up after yourselves no matter the situation. Just as we earn privileges, we take them away for breaking the golden rules. We are always kind to our brothers and sisters here in the community. If someone is unkind, you must report the infraction immediately."

"Oh, of course." Bree couldn't imagine that anyone would want to raise Blythe's hackles by breaking her golden rules.

"What we do out here isn't free, and everyone who comes here has to invest in our community. Are you willing to do that?" she asked.

"You mean you want us to give you money?" Mitch

asked, frowning.

"Yes, you'll need to pay to live here. Nobody gets to live and eat somewhere free. You'll be part of something bigger and paying your room and board is part of it. You'll also be paying for security and protection. Out here, you'll have no worries about safety. We pay people for that. We'll keep your cell phones out of an abundance of caution to carefully control who gains access to this community. None of us have secrets from the community. We are a family here. You'll need to fill out an application today and we'll review it."

"An application?" Mitch asked. "Like for a job?"

"More like for a loan or an apartment. You can't buy a house or get an apartment without providing sensitive information. If you're to live among us, we'll need to know everything about you."

Bree frowned. "Well, I guess that's fair enough, don't you think, honey?"

Mitch pretended to think about that for a few seconds. "Well, all right. We'll fill it out. But what happens if you don't want to let us in? If we don't have enough money or the right answers on the application?"

"Let's just worry about that if we come to it, okay?" Blythe's smile was pure honey. Bree suppressed a shudder. She'd seen that smile before, and nothing good came of it then.

"Gosh, I didn't know we'd have to take a test. I sure hope we pass. We've wanted to do this for so long." Bree threw herself into her character, knowing there was no other way to pull this off.

"How about we have a nice lunch before we worry any

more about that." Blythe indicated a table that had magically filled with food for four. She looked up and motioned to a slim, pretty brown-haired young woman who'd entered the building while they were talking. "We'll have my assistant, Joy, join us. She's just returned from a short trip.

"Joy, this is Michael and Jessica Lawson. They've just made the short trip from the Atlanta suburbs to join us. We'll need to have them fill out our application and waivers and such. Please join us for lunch so we can further discuss the particulars of life here in our little slice of heaven."

Joy pushed up her glasses and smiled. "It's so nice to meet you. Let me get Belinda to print up the paperwork and bring it over here while we eat."

"So, how was your trip, Joy?" Blythe asked.

Joy made eye contact with Blythe. "It was nice, thank you, but I didn't really get to see everything I'd hoped." Bree would've sworn something passed between the two women.

"I'd love to hear all about it. You can tell me more later." Blythe took a bite of what looked like a fresh broccoli salad.

"This looks delicious." Bree indicated the grilled chicken, baked sweet potato, and broccoli salad.

"Thank you. All of our food is whole food. We don't serve anything processed other than some breads we bake ourselves with the highest quality bread flours and grains."

"Well, honey. It looks like I'll lose a few pounds without my snacks." Bree elbowed Mitch lightly in the ribs.

"We like to make protein shakes with almonds, yogurt, and fruit. How do we get the ingredients for those?" Mitch asked.

"You'll have a kitchen to yourselves in your own cabin.

We'll have a lot of what you need here on hand as far as fresh fruit and dairy, but if there's something specific you want, there's a grocery list form. We do occasionally have to visit the store for certain items."

Mitch grinned. "Wow. No more shopping at the grocery store, baby. That's a level up right there." It was all Bree could do not to laugh out loud at Mitch's ability to slide into character so well.

Blythe smiled at Mitch like he was an eager puppy—kind of like he was cute but annoying at the same time. "You two enjoy your lunch. Joy and I are scheduled for a meeting in a few minutes. When you finish, Belinda will be on hand to direct you to the conference room where you can fill out your forms."

Blythe/Glynnis excused herself after wiping her mouth, leaving a smudge of pink lipstick on her napkin. Joy stuffed in another quick bite and shoved her chair back, eager to follow her boss from the dining hall.

That left Mitch and Bree staring after them. "I wonder what the quick exit was all about?" Bree took another bite of her lunch.

Mitch gave her a hard stare and mouthed the words *don't say anything—probably listening*. He pointed to his ear for effect.

Bree nodded. "Well, I sure hope we can stay since we've gone to all this trouble to get here." Might as well play the part as if someone were listening. She could understand why Blythe might want to get a sense of their character by listening to their conversation. Would their cabin be bugged as well? Gosh, she hoped not. That would make what they were trying to do much harder.

"We just have to do whatever it is they ask of us so they can't say no. I didn't think about paying them to let us stay here though. I hope it's not too expensive. I don't want to cut into our savings." Mitch likely added this so they would sound like any couple who were contemplating paying out money for an unknown and possibly expensive venture. "I wonder how much it costs?"

"Are you finished eating? I'm all done. The food was pretty good, but a little dessert would've made it better."

"Like you said, Jessi, we're probably gonna lose some weight while we're here if we can't have snacks. Maybe should've brought some with us, huh?"

They both stood and pushed in their chairs. "I guess we put our plates over there where Blythe and Joy put theirs." The two women had brought their plates over to a bin sitting on a tray on the side of the room. They'd scraped everything off the plates and emptied their water glasses into the bin, then they'd neatly stacked the plates, lined up the glasses, and laid the silverware to the side. Mitch and Bree followed suit.

They exited the dining hall into the sunshine. It was a few degrees cooler here because of the elevation and the breeze was nice.

A dark-haired woman appeared out of nowhere. "Hello, Michael and Jessica. I'm Belinda. Please follow so we can get your paperwork filled out."

"Oh, hi. Blythe said you would be waiting for us. It's nice to meet you." Bree looked for any signs of distress on Belinda's face. The woman appeared to be in her midthirties, trim, and eager to get them to the conference room.

They followed, looking around for whatever they could learn. So far, no one had spoken in their earpieces, which was a relief. Since everything they'd heard and saw was being streamed and recorded, the team would warn them of any dangers.

Again, a few other community members were walking here and there, but nobody stopped to say hello, despite their curious looks. Like the others, they were clean but plainly dressed in drab earth tones. Bree secretly wondered what would happen if somebody showed up to dinner dressed in bright red. It would be shocking, she'd just bet.

MITCH WAS TAKING it all in, watching and making mental notes about everything he saw and heard, but he realized something wasn't quite right with Bree. Her sudden intake of breath when she'd seen "Blythe" for the first time caught his attention. It was as if she'd recognized the woman, though he doubted that anyone else noticed Bree's response because she hadn't made a sound. Mitch had gotten to know her over the past couple of weeks working so closely together. He was again thankful for their disguises that would prevent anyone from recognizing them.

He felt pretty confident that all of their bank accounts, employment history, and other information they'd need to fill out on the forms would check out. The undercover GBI aliases were pretty airtight. The team wouldn't have handed them over to Mitch and Bree without working their magic on the backgrounds of them first. He and Bree both had a list of bank accounts and even online banking information on their phones. The passwords were listed in the notes section.

They'd need the phones to get that information. As soon as he could be sure they weren't being watched and listened to by the community, he'd tell the team what info they needed for the forms. It could all be fed to them through their earpieces, but most people wouldn't be able to pull up a bank account number without looking it up online, so he and Bree would ask for their phones back if that's what information was required.

It would be interesting to see how extensive the application was. Identity theft only required a few pieces of personal information. The team would be able to see what the forms looked like through their tech, so it was one more piece of evidence to add to the pile that seemed to be growing.

It would be helpful if they could speak to a few of the members of the community and ask them some questions. So far they seemed to view Mitch and Bree like new animals in the zoo. Of course the two of them had only been there less than two hours, so he figured once they'd gotten situated in their quarters and were introduced around, it would be easy to try and interact with others.

They arrived at what appeared to be a small office at the front of a larger building that Mitch knew to be the community hall where the group met for speeches by the leadership and daily sessions. According to Jimmy Lee, his momma liked to keep reminding everyone why they were there.

"We have a small conference room through here." Belinda indicated a doorway beyond the office where he noticed several posters on the wall with motivational quotes by famous people. He had to give it to them—they behaved in a professional manner and appeared to run things like a legitimate business. So far, if he hadn't known any better, he'd think they'd wound up in a fine place. Blythe had been at this kind of thing for quite a few years, so she'd figured it all out by now, he supposed.

There were six rolling office chairs around the rectangular table. There was a stack of paperwork neatly placed at each end of the table. "Here we go. Jessica, if you could sit here, and Michael over there."

Bree took her seat, and Mitch could tell she was a little nervous by the way her eyes darted to his. She immediately began reading over the forms. "Belinda, I don't have all of this information without looking it up on my phone. Do you think I could have it back so I can fill this out?" She blinked at Belinda with a wide-eyed, innocent stare.

"We don't expect you to have account numbers and such memorized, of course. Start with the personal information first, and then we can supply your phones for you to fill out the financial part of it."

"Oh, okay. Thanks."

Mitch looked down at the documents and found the pages they were to fill out first. A lot of it was stuff they'd already discussed—past employment, last address (which they'd both memorized down to the zip code), and the basics: age, sex, marital status, et cetera. And then there was an odd request: *Please write the name of your last closest neighbor and the color of their car.* Mitch immediately pulled out a pair of "reading glasses" that tech had slipped him at the last second.

He saw Bree chewing on her lip and recognized that she was stressed. As he put on the glasses, he focused on the one question they'd not addressed together about the neighbor. There was a brief pause and someone quickly came on and said, "Joe and Sue Bankman. He drove a black truck and she drove a red Prius." He saw Bree begin to fill out the questions quickly, knowing that she'd also heard the communication.

Someone entered the room holding both of their phones. Belinda stood in the corner of the room as if she were making sure they didn't "cheat" somehow. Mitch knew that there were cameras, possibly with audio, so trying to discuss any of their answers so far was out of the question.

"Can we collaborate on our answers for the financial part of things?" Bree asked. "Michael pays most of our bills online, and I'm not sure of some of the answers to these questions." Good on her for asking.

"Of course. You understand that we have to be careful when we have couples come in together and fill out personal information. We've had reporters working on undercover stories before. We just have to make sure that you really are who you say you are."

"Oh, we understand. Honey, can you scoot over here and help me fill this money stuff out? I don't know the answer to half of these questions." She sounded so authentic.

"Sure, Jessi." He stood and moved over beside her. They'd been handed their phones and were able to navigate getting online with the passwords that had been provided.

The form asked for Social Security number, driver's license number, bank account information, and any real estate they might own separately or together.

"I hope nobody's going to get access to this. It's enough to steal my identity three times over." Mitch laughed in a not so comfortable way. No wonder they'd been able to fleece the people who'd come here.

"Your private information stays private, so no worries about that. It's the same information you provide when you fill out a lease for an apartment or a home loan."

She was right about that, but in those situations nowadays, it was secure and online, so the employees didn't have unfettered access to the private information provided. He didn't say that though. "I guess you're right."

Once they were finished, Belinda collected their forms and their phones and smiled. "Blythe has really taken a liking to you two. She's suggested you join us for our afternoon meeting."

"Oh, yay. I'm so tickled to hear that. Aren't you, Michael?" Mitch put an arm around Bree and gave her a quick squeeze.

"You bet, honey. Just glad all that paperwork is done and we can get to learning about this place."

"The meeting area is right through here. It'll be about thirty minutes before things get started, so if you want to sit outside in the sunshine, you can do that while you wait."

Mitch was so relieved they would have a moment to talk without someone listening. "Sounds fantastic. It's such a nice area out there. Maybe we could have a walk around the green."

"Just be sure to stay around the grassy area. You don't yet have permission to move about the community freely."

"Gotcha. No problem. We'll just hang out there then."

Chapter Nineteen

B REE AND MITCH moved outdoors after filling out the requisite forms and paperwork as they'd been requested to do by Blythe, who was in fact Jimmy Lee's momma, Glynnis. As soon as they were finally alone, strolling together arm in arm, Bree quietly said, "Blythe is the same woman I met when I was a little girl—the one who threw Momma in a dark room alone for days on end when she was sobering up at our church. I can't believe it's her."

There was static in Bree's ear, startling her. "Bree, what was the name of the church where this happened?"

"The Followers of the Apostolic Faith. I'd forgotten her name but she has two different-colored eyes, so there's no way it's a mistake."

Mitch nodded. "I noticed that. You did good not letting her know that you recognized her."

Bree shrugged. "I was shocked—horrified really. But we've got a job to do, so I couldn't let it blow things."

Special Agent Roberts was in their ears. "It's a good clue. The two of you are broadcasting loud and clear. Help us get a look at some of the other members when you can so that we can run facial recognition. Information is coming in on some missing persons as reported by families that the police closed the files on due to lack of evidence or the fact that they'd left of their own volition."

Bree noticed that several members were beginning to converge to the larger building they'd just left. She nudged Mitch and pointed. "Looks like they're headed into the afternoon meeting."

"Keep up the good work, you two. Check back in when you can and keep in mind that any area can have listening devices. Cults use information they gather to manage their members and make them believe they have no freedom of speech, thought, or privacy, because they don't. So, be careful."

As they walked toward the gathering spot, Bree smiled at several members, both men and women, who smiled back tentatively. There seemed to be several couples and equally as many people walking alone. Inside, there was a small stage area with a mic set up and a couple of comfortable chairs. There looked to be around thirty plus folding chairs arranged in rows in a semicircle for the audience.

Mitch and Bree took seats a couple of rows back so they could see more of the members as they filled in the chairs. After a few minutes, they heard a tinkling sound like crystals being struck. It appeared that around twenty of the chairs were full, leaving a dozen or so empty.

Blythe approached the microphone and everyone got to their feet and began clapping—not cheering or whistling— just calmly clapping as if it were expected. There was no real enthusiasm in it though.

"Thanks, everyone. I'm happy to announce that we have visitors in our audience. Michael and Jessica Lawson are with us today." Blythe pointed toward Mitch and Bree, who waved. "They're hoping to become members of our humble group here at the Community of Atonement. I know you'll show them a warm welcome. While we process their paperwork, they'll be taking the tour."

A few members waved at them, and there was more bored clapping.

"A few housekeeping items. I've notice that a few of you left napkins on the tables at lunch today. Let's remember that this is your home, and as such, it's up to you to keep it clean and tidy. Since we have visitors, we won't name names today, but you know who you are."

Suddenly, Bree tried to remember what they'd done with their napkins. *Is she talking about us?* What happened to people who left their napkins on the table? A sense of foreboding crept up her spine. Were the members publicly shamed when they broke the rules? That sounded super creepy. After all, they weren't children. But then, she remembered what Blythe/Glynnis had done to her mother and to Jimmy Lee when he'd needed to be punished. The woman was ruthless.

As Bree looked around to gauge the response to Blythe's admonishment, she noticed the residents weren't making eye contact with each other as if nobody wanted to acknowledge the guilty. Had they all been guilty at one point or another and punished for it? Or just punished whether or not they'd been guilty so that they stayed in line?

Blythe pivoted subjects. "It's time again to begin the process of rending the sheep's wool. I've got a list of names of those who've been chosen to attend that task. Some of you helped with the shearing yesterday, so thank you. That group will move to crop harvesting. The corn is ready to pick and shuck, along with the peas. There's a lot of hot work to continue today. Remember to drink plenty of water and rotate out of the sun and reapply your sunscreen. Sunburn isn't an excuse to lie about."

Blythe began to read names and assign tasks. She finished with some kind of blessing for the crops and land, then there was another crystal tinkling sound and they were dismissed.

After everyone had begun to assemble into groups, Blythe approached Mitch and Bree. "Jessica, we'll let you head over to help out with picking sheep's wool. The other members will be happy to show you what to do. Oh, and Michael, you'll be picking corn this afternoon. Y'all will both need to wear sunscreen and sneakers or boots."

"Our suitcases are in the truck. Should I grab my shoes from there?" Bree asked.

"We've assigned you to cabin number five for now. Your things are already there, so follow the path there until you see the cabin. But hurry, so you don't get behind in your work. If you don't have your own sunscreen, we've got plenty at the workstations." She gave them a sweet smile. "I hope you aren't afraid of a day's work."

"No, ma'am. We're not," Mitch answered in his 'aw shucks' voice.

The truth was, Bree had no idea what rending sheep's wool entailed. It didn't sound particularly easy. "Where should we go once we get our things?"

"I'll have someone waiting outside to show you where to go."

Mitch and Bree headed in the direction where Blythe had pointed. As they followed the path, they were able to speak quietly, as nobody was close enough to hear. "Do you think this is a test?" she asked him.

"Most probably. Until they check out our answers on the forms. They likely want to test our mettle and see if we can do the dirty work around here."

"I'm not crazy about dirty work, but how bad can it be?"

TRUTH WAS, IT could be dirty and stinky and really pretty bad, Bree found out very quickly. It was a gross thing, all that wool. After it was shorn, it had to be washed, picked, and boiled. The smell alone turned her stomach. Bree hoped she was never in a situation where she had to spin her own thread from sheep's wool. For now, she would sit here and learn something new, despite the awful smell, and try to learn something about the other women who were working beside her.

There were six women gathered doing the dirty work outside beside the barn under an overhang of an aluminum shelter where bales of hay were kept. There was only a slight breeze here and the heat was oppressive. Bree was thankful for her shorter hair and for the clip she'd put it up in—and for the tech that clip provided.

A middle-aged woman sat closest to her, but so far, hadn't spoken to Bree. "Hi, I'm Jessica."

The woman looked up from her task. "I'm Patricia." She looked back down as she picked at the wool.

"How long have you been here?"

"'Bout two years, I guess."

"Do you like living here in the community?" Bree tried to make conversation but Patricia was making it hard.

The woman all but snorted, then she leaned in and said in a really low voice next to Bree's ear, "That's a real good question. You're new here, so you don't understand how things are yet, but if I were you, I'd get out while you still can—if you still can. Things aren't what they seem here."

Bree shifted her eyes toward Patricia's. "Are you okay?"

The woman shrugged her shoulders. "What's okay? I'm well fed, I've learned a lot of survival skills, and I don't have much to worry about as far as taking care of myself. So, I guess they kind of delivered on their promises."

"Yes, but are you *okay?*"

"Shh." Someone else made a shushing sound from nearby.

"They are always listening," Patricia whispered. "It's not likely they can hear us out here but be careful. You don't want to be punished for speaking your mind."

No, she did not. Bree shot Patricia a worried look.

"Punished? How?"

"Just follow the rules and don't go saying anything against the master or Blythe, or anybody else in a management role. Keep quiet and clean up after yourself. And don't ask so many questions." Patricia picked up her hank of wool that she'd been picking and moved away from Bree.

Bree looked down at the smelly wool in her hands and suddenly wondered why she hadn't heard anything about Sarah since she'd been here. According to Jimmy Lee, Sarah was somebody important in the community. Of course, Bree couldn't ask about her because she wasn't supposed to know anything except what she'd been told since arriving and the scant information available online.

A bead of sweat trickled downward between her shoulder blades to her waist. After she'd finished picking the wool clean, Bree returned it to the clean pile and took a sip of water from the reusable bottle she'd been provided. The water had a metallic taste and she longed for her filtered drinking water from home. This was most likely well water from the ground here in the community.

Not wanting to risk getting admonished by the other women, she sighed and grabbed another hank of wool from the dirty pile and got back to work. As she picked out the pieces of dirt, grass, and other unknown filth, Bree watched the other women from beneath her lashes, looking for any clues that might help them learn more about this odd place and the people in it.

MITCH ENJOYED A good workout as much as anybody, but picking corn wasn't so enjoyable. He hauled a wheelbarrow through the rows and filled it with corn from the tall, heavily laden stalks. He wore gloves and his hands were hot and sweaty inside. There were seven men and three women with him doing the same job. Nobody was talking to each other.

He'd tried to make small talk initially by introducing himself to a large man who went by the name of Joe. But Joe told him it was too hot to chat and work, so they should work. Mitch hoped he'd gotten a good look at Joe with his sunglasses that doubled as a camera. He tried to do the same with as many of the others as he could within his line of vision, but that was severely limited by the tightly planted rows of corn.

Mitch took a quick break to refill his water bottle and reapply sunscreen to the back of his neck under the small tent that was set up for the workers. There didn't seem to be anyone in charge or watching them do their jobs, but nobody appeared to lollygagging in their duties as far as Mitch could tell. It was like they didn't dare slack. Maybe they were all just really dedicated workers, or maybe they'd all learned the hard way that it was better to do as they were told. He did wonder about it.

Joe came over to refill his water bottle just as Mitch recapped the sunscreen. "Better get back to work. Don't want them to see you messing around."

"That right? How can they see us?" Mitch asked looking all around.

"Oh, they see us. Take my word for it." Joe capped his bottle and headed back out into the cornfield.

Mitch believed him. He'd seen the fear in Joe's eyes. So, he spent the next two hours picking corn until he'd dumped and refilled the heavy wheelbarrow countless times. Until the shadows lengthened and his back began to ache. Finally, a whistle sounded and the others began to come in from the field. He wondered if picking sheep's wool had been any better for Bree. He certainly hoped she'd been able to gather more intel in the hours she'd worked than he had.

BREE WAS EXHAUSTED in a way she hadn't been in ages. By the time she and Mitch met up for dinner after their shifts had ended, she could tell he was as worn out as she was. "You okay?" she asked.

"Yeah. You?" He nodded, but she could tell he'd had a long day in the sun. His cheeks were red from the heat. She hoped he hadn't gotten sunburned under the baseball cap he'd worn.

They entered the mess hall with the other members, all of whom appeared too hot and tired and hungry to exchange pleasantries. They ate, cleaned up their tables, and then followed the others into the assembly area for end-of-day announcements as the sun was setting.

Blythe thanked them for their hard work, reminding them that hard work was indeed a blessing and benefited everyone. She announced in an excited voice that the master would be paying them a visit in the coming days and reminded everyone to make sure everything was especially clean, and to keep their eyes averted when in his presence.

"Spoken like a true cult maven," Bree whispered under her breath. Bree thought this was really odd and frankly very cultish to suggest that anyone treat another person as if they were too special to look upon directly, but of course she kept from rolling her eyes and snorting as she figured it wouldn't go over well.

It was strange how quickly Bree felt like she was part of this community. This burdened, controlled, and anxious group of people who'd found themselves together and had no idea how to get out. She had to remind herself that they weren't stuck like the others and that they were actually here to free these people, despite the fact that they'd all come here of their own free will.

Chapter Twenty

MICHAEL AND JESSICA Lawson were welcomed into the Community of Atonement by Belinda right after coming in from their workstations later that evening as they were preparing to head into the cafeteria. Their paperwork had checked out, apparently. The discussion about how much money would be taken from their joint checking account to pay for their expenses and help fund the community hadn't yet taken place.

Mitch and Bree played up their excitement over being accepted and pretended to be overjoyed when they got word. Mitch knew that any sane and rational person would ask about the money, so after dinner and a day as a field hand shucking corn, he broached the subject with Blythe. He caught her right as she was about to address the group at day's end.

"Oh, Blythe, Jess and I were wondering how much it's going to cost us to live here monthly. We've been saving to buy a house and want to make sure it's not more than we can afford." He all but stood in her way to keep her from brushing past him.

"I really don't have time to discuss this right now. You should make an appointment with Belinda on Saturday. She has the numbers."

"But this is our money and we need to know how much it will cost. No one has given us an amount yet. We can't stay here if we can't afford it." Mitch stood his ground.

Blythe seemed to grow two feet taller and suddenly take up a lot more space. "You haven't been here long enough to understand how things run here, Michael, but it's time you learned. If I say that I don't have time to discuss this matter right now, you move along and don't press the issue. The two of you came here because you wanted to join our community. I told you it wouldn't be cheap or free, and that you had to follow our rules. Not following rules has consequences. Ask around and then decide if you want to make waves." There was an unspoken threat in her tone. She then stepped around Mitch and ignored Bree.

Mitch met Bree's gaze. The rubber had met the road now, and the woman was showing her true stripes. They'd already known about those stripes and it was almost a relief to him for her to reveal herself finally. "There she is." Mitch said this under his breath, and he could tell that Bree had heard him when she nodded.

Once they were in their cabin, Mitch realized the awkwardness of their situation. They would have to sleep in the same bed. There was a tiny kitchenette with a sink, microwave, toaster, blender, and fridge. Two chairs sat on either side of a small table with a lamp between them. "You can take the first shower if you want." He motioned to the tiny bathroom that barely had room for one person.

"Thanks." She smiled, but it wasn't her usual light-up-the-room kind of smile. She disappeared into the small bathroom while Mitch made some encrypted notes in his small notebook. He'd learned years ago to make his notes non sensible to others by rearranging the words just so. He had a system that only he could read. He'd looked around the room for cameras but hadn't seen any, but he was pretty sure there were listening devices—had to assume there were. Those were much harder to spot. Plus, the team was always listening.

Bree emerged wearing a robe over a pair of pajamas. The top was sleeveless and the bottoms were shorts. The small one-room cabin was air-conditioned but still warm, so she'd planned well. He couldn't help but admire her toned arms and legs though, and now he wouldn't be able to unsee them. Hopefully, he'd fall asleep immediately and not lie awake thinking about her sexy body next to him all night.

"All yours."

"Thanks, babe." He tried to keep up their couple's banter just in case somebody was listening. "Feel better?"

"Like a new person. I've never smelled anything quite so stinky as boiled sheep's wool right after it's been sheared. I don't recommend." She wrinkled her nose.

"I'm not sure which is less fun, picking corn all day or shucking it—which is what I'll be doing tomorrow. I had no idea this is what coming here would be like. I wonder what's next."

"I'm guessing a good night's sleep is next for both of us after you get cleaned up. I'll say good night, honey. I'm whipped." She pulled the towel off her wet hair and fluffed it and then climbed into bed.

"Mmm, night. I'm right behind you. I'll try not to wake

you if you're asleep when I'm done."

This kind of communication felt strange and awkward. They were saying what they needed to say, but not able to say what they wanted or able to discuss either of their feelings about the day and what had occurred. Somehow they'd need to find a way to share information.

BREE FELL INTO bed after her shower, physically exhausted. There were so many things she wanted to discuss with Mitch but felt as if someone had put a gag on her. Being a therapist meant talking things out and expressing feelings. She felt like she would explode keeping her thoughts in like this every day they were here. It was maddening. Not maddening enough not to fall into a deep, coma-like sleep however, because the next thing she knew, Mitch was shaking her gently awake. "Jess. It's time to wake up. It's six o'clock."

"Six? We don't get up at six," she mumbled.

"Now we do, sweetie."

Bree stretched her legs and her toes brushed a hairy calf muscle. She pulled her foot back like she'd been burned. She turned her head to peek at Mitch. His blond bedhead and shirtless chest made her groan. "I need coffee."

"Got some brewing. Good thing coffee is considered a whole food, huh?" He grinned and her insides responded. *Oh dear.* She quickly rolled to the opposite side of the bed and climbed out.

"This is way too early for me." Bree yawned to cover her discomfort. Plus, she had to pee, so she headed to the bathroom. Touching his bare leg had woken her up in a way that no coffee could've.

Once they'd had a quick cup of coffee and gotten dressed, Bree tamed her hair as best she could after sleeping with it wet. Then they headed outside to gather with the other residents near the center of the green with a few minutes to spare. They'd been told that's where everyone went to start their day.

Blythe was there, looking like she'd been up for hours, showered, hair styled and makeup perfect. Bree wondered at her age because the woman had great skin and hair for someone who'd live as long as they all knew she had to have a son Jimmy Lee's age. Plus, she was probably around the same age as Bree's momma, given that they'd met when she was a child.

There was a set of steps that led up to a small raised out-door platform of sorts. Blythe did like her stages, it appeared. She also wasn't a stranger to a microphone, which she clutched while one of her lackeys stood nearby and held the small portable amp that it required. "Good morning, community. I'm glad to see that y'all are up and ready to start your day as the sun rises on our beautiful land. We'll head into breakfast soon, but first I wanted to let you know that the master will arrive today, so I'm warning you to be on your very best behavior. You know what that means, friends, so let's show him our appreciation for all that he does for us."

Bree heard a few scoffs and snorts around her, though she couldn't quite pinpoint who they'd come from. Blythe narrowed her eyes and her face flushed, so obviously she'd heard them too. "You don't want the punishment that's coming your way should you embarrass yourself in front of the master, so maintain your dignity and keep your distance. Eyes down." She played the tinkling crystal sound. "Dismissed."

"Sounds like she's nervous that someone might embarrass her in front of the master. Like a school principal when the board supervisor comes for a visit and the kids act up." Bree said this softly in Mitch's ear as they moved from the green area to the cafeteria for breakfast.

"Yeah. She did sound worried and very threatening. And it seems like more than one person is disgruntled enough to make a stink and embarrass her. I'm looking forward to getting a look at the master."

"Me too. I wonder if he's kind of like Jim Jones or David Koresh." Bree named two of the most historically notorious cult leaders.

"Let's hope not. Maybe 'the master' has Blythe under his control. It's the first time she's appeared worried or nervous since we've met her. Maybe she's afraid of him. Sounds like she's tasked with keeping the members in line and making sure things run smoothly. Maybe she gets 'punished' if the members don't behave."

"Maybe so. It definitely bears watching." They fell in line for the breakfast buffet that included scrambled eggs, bacon, grits, hash brown potatoes, and coffee.

"At least we won't starve here. I guess if you're going to run a cult, you'd better feed your members well at least." Bree sat down next to a woman who eyed her suspiciously.

"Hi, I'm Jessica. We haven't met yet." Bree was wearing

the camera pendant that looked like a crystal. Every time she encountered someone new, she introduced herself and forced the person to tell her their name so that the team could get a good photo of them to try to help identify as many missing persons as possible in the community.

"I'm Charity." But Charity didn't appear thrilled to meet her.

"How long have you been in the community, Charity?" Bree flashed her a big smile.

"Just over a year." She kind of mumbled her answer and cast her eyes downward.

"This is my husband, Michael." She introduced Mitch, who waved and smiled at Charity.

"Ya'll seem nice. I hope things go well for you." Charity picked up her plate and moved to a different table without saying another word.

That left the two of them sitting with another couple across the table, both of whom avoided Bree and Mitch's eyes. "Looks like nobody wants to talk to us." That had been the prevailing behavior of the other members since they'd arrived yesterday. Whatever had happened to these folks while they'd been here, they'd learned it was best to keep to themselves and not get friendly with others. Because nobody appeared to be socializing with one another.

"That's okay, darlin', we can keep each other company for now. They'll learn to love us. What's not to like?" Mitch shot her a grin and elbowed her gently in a joking fashion. It was hard to believe that he struggled socially when watching him playing this role. It was as if he'd watched lots of movies and television and had learned how to mimic characters he'd seen.

They finished eating, cleaned up, and headed outside, not exactly eager for what the day might bring regarding the hot sun and manual labor, but both were resigned to it for the greater good. Today appeared to be more of the same kind of work as yesterday, and with it a chance to learn more about the members and gather evidence. The more they heard and saw, the better their chances to find one or more clues that would end this investigation in their favor.

MITCH KNEW THEY would need to figure out a way to get into some of the places around the compound where they'd not been thus far. Being new and seemingly ignorant of the rules might come in handy to "accidentally" stumble into a building or two. Maybe breaking one or two of those rules could get him someplace where they could discover more evidence. But they'd need to walk a fine line because they couldn't blow the case before getting the information they needed to nail down a conviction.

Mitch pulled on the dirty pair of work gloves he'd been given yesterday and donned the baseball cap after liberally applying sunscreen to his ears, neck, hands, and face. Today, he wore a long-sleeved western-style shirt with jeans so that he was protected from the sun. They were supposed to be shucking corn today instead of picking it, but he wanted to be prepared for whatever the day brought. Mitch noticed that Bree was also better dressed for a day's work outdoors this morning, wearing a wide-brimmed sun hat with a long-sleeved button-up linen shirt and jeans with sneakers. She'd also loaded up on sunscreen before they'd left the cabin.

Just as they were about to head their separate ways to work, Belinda approached them. "Hi, Jessica. Blythe wanted me to grab you before you headed out to the barn. She says your application said you'd had some experience with office work and spreadsheets. We're updating our files and hoped you might be able to help us with some of the data entry."

Mitch watched Bree's eyes carefully. He really had no idea how much experience she actually had working with spreadsheets and computers, so he wanted to be sure she wouldn't blow her cover if she helped them out.

"I think you just saved my life. I love a good spread-sheet—a whole lot more than picking dirt from sheep's wool. I'd be thrilled to help out. I'm hoping y'all have air-conditioning where I'm to work?" She grinned from ear to ear.

Mitch breathed a silent sigh of relief. She sounded completely confident, and even better, it would hopefully give her the opportunity to lay eyes on some of the community's information and records. He hoped her pendant would be able to capture the screen in front of her so the special agents back at the sheriff's office could see what she saw in real time.

Even if Bree didn't know spreadsheets, he figured one of the tech people could walk her through it using the listening device in her ear. Of course, that would be a lot harder, so he was hoping she had at least rudimentary knowledge of whatever it was they wanted her to do.

"Oh, good. And yes, there is air-conditioning. Come with me."

"Bye, honey. I guess I'll see you back here at lunchtime." Mitch winked at her and she blew him a kiss. "Enjoy the air-conditioning." He noticed a few dirty looks cast Bree's way at his words.

Mitch headed toward the Jeep that he assumed would take him out to the cornfield. As he climbed in he recognized a couple of the guys from yesterday, including Joe, whom he'd met and tried to make conversation with. Mitch nodded at the men. They nodded in return, but Joe avoided Mitch's eyes.

Their driver said, "Today, we're shucking corn at the barn, so it won't be quite so hot as out in the field yesterday. We'll have shade at least part of the day. They try to keep us from getting too smelly and dirty when the master comes around for a visit."

"Why is that?" Mitch asked.

"He likes to think everything here just appears like magic. That we don't have to work like slaves to make it happen. If he sees us like we were yesterday, it tweaks his conscience." The man who said this wasn't someone that Mitch had met previously.

Joe shushed him. "Dan, you better keep your opinions to yourself."

"We'd all better keep our opinions to ourselves, unless we want to get punished. And I don't think speaking our minds is worth that, do you?" the driver said. "I mean, has anybody seen Sarah since she got into that fight with Blythe?"

The others shook their heads and looked down, avoiding any further discussion of the master or mind-speaking or the missing Sarah.

Mitch wanted to ask questions, but had the feeling it would only lead to more unrest, so for now, he kept quiet. But he had the feeling Dan might be someone who'd welcome a conversation at a later time. And where had Sarah gone? Did Blythe have something to do with her leaving? He'd thought it was strange that nobody had mentioned her name since they'd been there. Jimmy Lee had talked about her like she was somebody who'd been in charge of things alongside his momma.

Once Mitch made it to the barn, he moved away from the others just far enough to mutter where the team could hear. "Ask Jimmy Lee if he knew about a fight between his momma and Sarah, and if she left before or after him, or before Jolene, for that matter."

"Copy." The tech team was quiet mostly, so he'd gotten used to having the earpiece in his ear without hearing any feedback. Hearing the response was good for his peace of mind.

Something about the Sarah thing was clicking in his head. The pieces weren't fitting together just right, and he wasn't sure what it was that had him rattled—besides all of it. The whole idea of "the master" was weird and creepy enough, but these grown men and women being afraid to speak to each other for fear of retribution the likes of possibly a mysterious disappearance had Mitch wondering what they'd done to these poor souls besides keeping them here and stealing their money.

It suddenly made him nervous that Bree had been singled out like that with no warning. Surely she wasn't the only one here with business training and computer skills. He spoke quietly as he turned away from the others. "Keep an eye on Bree. Something is making me nervous about them taking her aside like that."

"Copy."

Chapter Twenty-One

B REE FOLLOWED BELINDA into the office, half relieved that she didn't have to spend the day outside in the hot, humid, and buggy summer day picking grit from sheep's wool, but half wondering why they'd singled her out for office work.

Data entry was essentially typing, and any middle schooler could do that. Why the special treatment on her second day? Surely, this would be a privilege saved for someone who'd earned it in the community, not a newcomer who had yet to pay her dues. Something about this didn't sit right with Bree and it made her nervous.

Belinda was biting her lip as if she was frustrated, instead of behaving in her usual calm manner. "Wait here." She pointed to the same conference table where she and Mitch had filled out their forms the day before. Then, Belinda left the room. Bree knew she was likely on camera, so she didn't move or speak, but she heard someone in her earpiece say quietly, "We're here with you, Bree."

Bree was relieved to hear the voice. Relieved to not feel alone in the moment. Something was happening here and she was afraid it wasn't going to go well for her. At least she had the team listening and watching, ready to come to her aid should she need them.

On edge, she tried not to fidget. Bree had a habit of bouncing her knee when she was nervous—a throwback from childhood. Her sister, Darla, still twirled her hair. Both girls had had some real anxiety from a young age. As an adult, she'd learned through her psychological training how her childhood fears and worries had formed her, and she'd been able to work through some of the trauma from her mother's alcoholism and her father's abandonment.

Right now, the unknown was bearing down on Bree, and it felt much like it had when Momma had gone off on a bender. Anything could happen, and none of it was likely to be something good.

The room was cold, and she was glad to have long sleeves on, despite the heat outside. Why were they making her sit and squirm? What was going on? She heard a loud click in her earpiece. Before, she could hear a slight buzz, but it was like it had gone dead. She wanted to tap it and ask if anybody was there. But somehow she knew they weren't. A cold dread seized her.

She stood and walked to the door, prepared to open it. It was locked from the other side. She knocked. "Hello? I need to use the bathroom. Could somebody let me out?"

Nobody answered. The room suddenly went dark. Pitch-dark because there wasn't a window. Panic clawed at Bree. She banged on the door harder. "Hello? Somebody help me."

The next few minutes were pure chaos.

The door opened, knocking her backward. Someone roughly pulled her up to standing, tied some kind of blindfold around her eyes, and pulled her hands behind her back and secured them with what must've been a zip tie. "Be quiet, or you'll regret it," a woman's voice rasped in her ear. A piece of tape was slapped on her mouth, duct tape most likely.

Bree was so shocked, she didn't have the courage to respond in that moment. Someone pushed her roughly out the door and she listened to hear if the team was back online, but they weren't, so she tried to pay close attention to where she was going, using her mental map they'd gone over and over of the compound to help figure out where they were taking her.

They ripped off her necklace and hat. Today she wasn't wearing the camera hair clip, so that didn't help. She still had the glasses in her pocket, and she wasn't sure if they had any kind of location tech in them or they only had a camera/video.

Bree was shoved into a car—a van maybe—and driven on a curvy, bouncy dirt road for about twenty minutes. She thought she might be sick from the motion, but the vehicle stopped just before it came to that. There were two voices, a man and a woman's. Belinda's and one she didn't recognize.

She wondered if they'd discovered they were undercover. What about Mitch? Bree was terrified they would hurt him. Would they bring him to where she was? Would the team come and find them?

Someone pulled her out of the vehicle rather roughly. "C'mon. The master wants to see you."

Bree was brought from the hot outdoors into a cool interior that smelled like pipe smoke. A home? She didn't have to wait long to find out because the blindfold was taken off and she was plopped into a deep leather chair. Looking around, Bree noticed that this was someone's living room. A nice one with a long wall of windows with a gorgeous view. The house sat on the side of the mountain and overlooked miles of forest and streams. The décor was masculine with lots of wood and leather with high ceilings and modern fixtures.

"How do you like my home?"

Bree's head snapped around at the sound of that voice. The one she remembered so well from her childhood. "Daddy?" The word was ripped from her heart.

"You look so much like your sister. But you tried to change yourself so we wouldn't recognize you. Did you think you could hide your identity from me? Your father?" The man who stood in front of her was older than the father she remembered. But he was her daddy.

"Why…how?" Bree didn't know what to say first. There were so many questions—all the questions she'd been asking herself since the day he'd walked out of their lives when she was ten years old. Tears were rolling down her cheeks.

He still had the same thick hair parted on the side, but it wasn't dark anymore; instead it had turned salt and pepper. Bernard Edward Hawthorne. Her momma had called him Ed. The master. The deserter. The ruiner of hers and Darla's childhoods, along with making Momma's alcoholism worse by leaving her alone and helpless to struggle with two young daughters without his emotional and financial support.

Daddy let out what sounded like a long-suffering sigh. "I know you probably have questions, Bree. You always were a curious little thing—so serious. How's your sister, Darla? Gosh, I hardly remember what she looked like. It was so long ago. But you—I couldn't ever get those accusing blue eyes out of my head. Are you wearing contacts?"

"You just said I looked so much like Darla, but you hardly remember her?" Bree was beginning to think she was losing her mind. Or maybe he was.

He laughed. "Oh, you don't know, do you? I was talking about your sister, Sarah. Your younger sister. The two of you look so much alike now that you've dyed your hair. We call her Sarah because she's always been so big for her britches. Such a handful—she always was." His eyes filled with emotion and love as he spoke about her—*sister*?

"We have a sister?" Bree was hanging on by a thread now. "Where is she?" Nobody had mentioned Sarah since she'd been there.

"She's been gone from here for a while. She and Glynnis didn't exactly get along, so Sarah went out on her own to find herself like young people do sometimes, I guess. I get texts from her every now and then letting me know she's off having adventures." But Bree could tell that he was concerned for her by his manner.

"How long has she been gone?" Bree asked.

"Too long, honestly. I thought she'd have come home by now." He frowned, gazing off into the distance out the window, then suddenly as if he realized where he was, he regained his focus, looking directly at Bree. "Now, it's time for you to tell me why you're here trying to ruin what I've built."

Bree had to be careful. Say the right thing. As much as

WHAT THEY DON'T KNOW

she longed to scream at him, she didn't know what frame of mind he might be in. "I'm not here to ruin anything. I've been looking for you all of my adulthood, Daddy. I can't believe I've finally found you."

His eyes softened for a moment. "I hated leaving you girls behind with your momma like that but she needed you and you needed her. Y'all were too young to come with me on my life's journey."

"Why *did* you need to leave us behind?" Bree tried to sound like a hurt child instead of the very angry woman she now was becoming.

"I had a life to live, and staying with your mother was a real drag. That woman never would've gotten herself right. Plus, I met Glynnis, and we were of the same mind. She's been with me every step of the way."

"You married her? Is she Sarah's mother?" Bree's mind was nearly spinning with confusion.

He laughed then. "Marry Glynnis? Goodness, no. I've got children with other women, but not Glynnis. She's got a no-good son who's gone off to God knows where." He waved a dismissive hand referencing Jimmy Lee. "I'll have to introduce you to your other sisters one day. They're sweet. No, I never married again after the trainwreck of a marriage I had with your mother. Learned my lesson there."

"Where did you go, Daddy? We missed you." It was a simple question followed by a simple statement. Both of which she'd hoped to utter to him someday.

"Oh, here and there. I moved around some, got my education, learned about life and people and what's important." He sounded righteous. As if leaving his two little girls and struggling wife had been the better decision.

"What was more important than your family?" Bree asked, unintentionally revealing that hurt child she'd been her entire life. "Than Darla and me—and Momma?"

His gaze lit on her again and became suddenly dark. "Don't judge me, young lady. I remember how you looked at me. Shaming me." But as quickly as he angered, his eyes cleared and the mask of calm reclaimed his features. "Tell me what you know about our community. And tell me who you've told about us. We've jammed your communications and moved you to our safe house where nobody will find you. Oh, and your young man is with us here as well. I'll assume his name isn't Michael."

"I was trying to find you. We didn't want to come here without backup. Our friend is in tech, so he hooked us up with a couple of listening devices just in case things didn't go well. The Community of Atonement has a reputation online as a cult. But we weren't sure what kind, so we thought it was better to be safe than sorry if it was the bad kind of cult."

"How did you find me? I don't use my name anywhere." He'd grabbed hold of her shoulder and was squeezing pretty hard. She winced and he let go. "Sorry."

"We met Jimmy Lee Monroe, Glynnis's son. He's been looking for his missing wife, Jolene, and he told us about this place and about you. When he said that his momma had one brown eye and one blue eye and described a man they called the master, I knew it had to be you, Daddy."

"Did he tell you that we have no idea where Jolene is? That he ran off shortly after she left and Glynnis can't find him?"

Bree nodded. "He's worried about Jolene. Says she and Glynnis didn't get along."

"Does he think Glynnis did something to her?"

Bree shrugged. "He's not sure."

"So he sent you here to spy on us to see if you could find out anything about Jolene?"

Bree nodded, going with it. "It gave me an excuse to find you finally. People talk to me, Daddy, because I'm a therapist. That's how I met Jimmy Lee." If he thought that she and Mitch were here on their own and not with a larger police investigation, maybe he wouldn't totally freak out and think he was in some kind of deep trouble, which he totally was.

"I know. I've kept up with you and your sister." He shifted in his chair. "Jimmy Lee was worried that Glynnis would keep him here against his will and he wouldn't be able to look for Jolene."

"Did he tell you that you wouldn't be able to leave once you got inside the community?" Daddy asked.

"Jimmy Lee told us only what he wanted us to know to get information from us. I guess he left that part out. Said his momma would only keep *him* here against his will. But he knew we wanted to get inside to find you, so it would benefit us both."

"What did you think would happen once you found me, little girl?"

Bree didn't have an answer for that. After all, she'd been making this all up as she went along, hopefully buying time while the team found them. *If* the team found them. She hung her head. "I—I really don't know, Daddy. I've wondered my whole life why you left us and where you went. I finally got the first real clue as to where you were, so we made a plan with Jimmy Lee and Mitch, and I headed here to find you."

"Now what am I going to do with the two of you?" he asked.

"The first thing you're going to do is get her to tell me where the hell my son is." Glynnis, a.k.a. Blythe, came striding through the door holding a revolver.

"Glynnis, put that gun down. There's no need for violence."

"I'm tired of you telling me what to do, *Master*. I've sat back and allowed it for the last twenty-five years, and I'm done with you chasing skirts while I handle all of the hard work and you get the glory and respect. Do you know how many beatings I've given out on your behalf? How many of our members I've shut in the dark for days on end because they dared question our methods? Or you?"

Bernard Edward Hawthorne appeared completely shocked at hearing Glynnis revealing her methods of running their cult. "You abused our people?"

"Oh, don't act so shocked. How do you think we keep them in line so we can take their money? Do you think they donate their worldly possessions willingly?"

"Well, I knew we had to manipulate them a bit here and there. It's a cult, after all. They are here to be influenced because they can't handle the real world. They need us to tell them what to do. They need us and we need them." All of a sudden, he didn't seem like the bad guy anymore, just the patsy, with Glynnis calling the shots.

Bree didn't know whether to be scared or to laugh at them. This was ridiculous. Her father the cult leader was utterly ridiculous. She had sisters she hadn't known about. And Glynnis was still holding the gun.

"Enough of this. Where is Jimmy Lee?" Glynnis demanded, now pointing the gun at Bree. She didn't appear to be kidding around either.

"I'll tell you if you tell me what happened to Jolene. That's what he sent us here to find out." Bree decided to stick to that story for now.

"I have no idea what happened to that little hussy. She took off and left my boy in the dust. Poor baby. Him with mental health challenges and all." Her response was so honest without a hint of hesitation.

Suddenly, Bree understood. "Tell me what happened to Sarah if you want to know where Jimmy Lee is."

The woman's eyes shifted first to her and then to Daddy. Guilt. "How would I know? She took off and never came back. Ed gets texts from her now and again, don't you, Ed?"

"I've never believed those texts were from Sarah."

"What? That's ridiculous. Who else would they be from?" She didn't make eye contact with either of them. Bree knew human behavior. Glynnis was responsible for Sarah's disappearance. But not Jolene's.

"Glynnis, did you do something to Sarah?" Daddy's voice was low and ominous.

"Of course not, Ed. I loved Sarah. I'd never hurt her." Despite wielding a gun, Glynnis cowered, her voice losing its bravado.

Bree knew without a doubt that nothing good was about

to go down. She thought she saw a flash off to the side through the window, and there was a series of loud bangs, booms, and smashes as figures dressed all in black in riot gear crashed through the front door and what seemed like all of the windows at once. The team had found them.

"She has a gun," Bree yelled loudly and pointed toward Glynnis. But someone had already relieved her of her weapon and put Glynnis face down on the floor with her hands behind her back. The same with Daddy.

"Are you all right?" one of the team members asked. She hadn't learned all of their names—hadn't even met them all.

"Have they found Mitch? Is he okay?" she asked.

He nodded. "Affirmative. He's just outside if you want to see him."

Bree hadn't ever wanted to see anyone as much as she did Mitch at this moment. She nearly ran the poor guy over trying to get out of there, barely sparing her father a glance on the way out. She would deal with him later.

The second she exited, Bree looked all around, spotting Mitch. Someone was bandaging a bloody wound on his forehead. "Are you all right?"

He reached for her the second he saw her. "Did they hurt you?"

"No, I'm okay. Did they tell you? The master. He's my daddy, Mitch."

Chapter Twenty-Two

THEY STEPPED OUT of the police vehicle into the humid late afternoon in Moonshine. Chase greeted them at the door. "Are you two okay?"

Bree appeared to still be a little stunned by everything that had happened back at the compound, and Mitch's head was hurting like hell. "We're okay. There's a lot to tell you though."

"We've got Jimmy Lee back here to help us fill some of this in. He's worried about his momma too. Wants to know what happened."

An agent brought Mitch's phone to him. "It's been ringing like crazy the past hour. Same number over and over."

Mitch looked down at the device and answered. "Hello?"

"Mitch. Kevin at the forensics lab. We just got the DNA back on your body from the gravel pit. It's not Jolene Monroe."

Something slid into place for Mitch in that moment. "Thanks for letting me know. Any hits on who it might be?"

"Not yet. Do you find out anything?"

"Maybe. I've got an idea who she is. I'll call you back in a few minutes."

Mitch turned to Bree, who had only heard his end of the

conversation. "It's not Jolene's body."

Bree's eyes were sad. "It's got to be Sarah. Sarah from the community. She and Glynnis had a fight and Sarah supposedly ran off and never came back. She and Daddy were arguing about it when the team came in. Oh, and Sarah was my sister. Daddy loved her." Bree whispered the last two words as if she didn't have the energy to finish the sentence.

Mitch put an arm around her. "I'm so sorry, Bree. But I've got to go to work now. We're going to get justice for Sarah, okay? I wish I could stay with you. I know it's been a tough few days."

He could see the exhaustion and emotion in her gaze. She looked like she was about to break. "No. It's okay. I just need to call my sister. She needs to know what's happening."

"Give me her number."

Bree found the number and handed him her phone without another word. Mitch handed Bree off to Hannah, who'd magically appeared with a concerned expression on her face. "C'mon, let's find out how Tiny's doing."

Mitch called the number for Bree's sister, Darla.

"Bree? Is everything okay?"

"Hi, Darla, this is Mitch Calloway, Bree's friend—"

"Where's Bree? Is she okay? Where's my sister?" He could hear panic in her voice.

"She's okay. Everything is fine. Bree's completely unharmed, but she's had a bit of a shock, and I was hoping you might be able to come out here and be with her. The two of you should be together right now."

"Why? What's happened?"

"Darla, we've found your father. He's in good health but

he's been living and running a cult in the mountains. Bree and I went looking for someone there and we found him instead."

There was a moment of silence. "You found Daddy at a cult? He's a cult *leader*?" Darla began to laugh hysterically.

"Are you all right? Should I send someone to pick you up? Where are you?" Mitch was very concerned for Bree's little sister in that moment. Maybe he shouldn't have told her.

The laughter stopped. "Poor Bree. She worried and wondered and questioned all these years. She was two years older than me, so I hardly remembered him, but Bree did. I wasn't emotionally attached to him. She was. I'm on my way. I'm sorry for laughing, but it's just so absurd that he's been running a cult all these years. I hope he didn't hurt anyone."

"We're looking into that. He's in police custody now."

"At least we know he's not dead. How's Bree holding up?"

"She's been through an ordeal. The shock of seeing him again so unexpectedly has kind of knocked the wind out of her. She needs rest and she needs her sister." He didn't mention the other sister. That would be a conversation between the two of them.

"Yes, she does. I'll be there in about three and a half hours."

"I'll let her know. We'll get her back with Tiny until you arrive. That should help."

"Definitely. See you soon."

Mitch just wanted to get back to work. All of this emotional turmoil was grinding on him, despite the fact that he knew it was all for Bree's benefit. He approached Bree where she was sitting next to Hannah's desk. "I'll call Sadie and get her to bring Tiny over here. Darla is on her way. She'll be here in a few hours."

Bree looked up at him. She'd taken the brown contacts out and her blue eyes were startling. "Thank you, Mitch."

"Okay. I'll see you later."

He knew that when Darla arrived, they would have a lot to get through. Finding out they had a sister they never knew and now wouldn't ever meet would be a tough thing. Living with the fact that their father had not only left them as little girls but had also gone on to have more children whom he loved more had to be crushing.

He'd lost his father's love through no fault of his own and it was beyond crushing, so he had some idea of what it was like.

Now, he had to focus on being the ace investigator he was known to be. The next mystery to solve was: Where was Jolene Monroe? It was time to speak to Jimmy Lee and see what he had to say now that they had this new information.

SADIE BROUGHT TINY over to her almost immediately, and Bree nearly burst into tears at seeing him. Tiny licked her face and wagged his tail with pure glee at seeing her. "I'm here, sweetie. Mommy's back." She cuddled him until he settled.

"Thanks so much for keeping him, Sadie."

"He was a delight. Poor Daisy Mae will miss him so much. In fact, I'm going to have to consider finding her a permanent playmate now that I've seen how happy she's been with Tiny over the past couple of days."

"I'll stop by and pick up his things tomorrow."

"No need. I've got his bag sitting right outside. I knew you might be tired when you got back. Is everything okay?" she asked, searching Bree's face.

"Not exactly okay. A long story really, but I'll explain what's happened once I can better understand it myself in a few days. My sister, Darla, is driving in from Huntsville this evening, so the two of us will spend some time together figuring things out."

"Let me know if I can help, okay?" Bree knew that Sadie meant it. After everything she'd been through, Sadie understood emotional struggle.

"I will. Thanks. Right now, I'm going to take Tiny home and cuddle with him—after I take a long, hot bath."

Bree thanked Hannah for her help as well. She looked around for Mitch and was told that he was in an interview room with Jimmy Lee. Part of her felt like she should be sitting shoulder to shoulder with him, continuing the work on this case, but she didn't have the heart right now. Maybe tomorrow.

"Oh, Bree, can you stop by tomorrow so that we can debrief you?" Aaron Roberts caught her as she was about to leave.

"Uh, sure. I'm sure this is all confusing for everyone."

"We've got your father in lockup here if you want to see him."

"Maybe when I come in tomorrow. My sister will be with me, and before today, neither of us had seen him since we were young children. So, this is pretty complicated."

"If we'd had any idea this would become personal, you never would've been allowed to participate in the investigation. This kind of coincidence is very rare. But we'll need to get as much information as possible to get convictions. I hope you understand. Can we count on you to work with us?"

Bree felt like she'd been punched. "You need me to work him for information?"

"He might be willing to tell you something that he won't reveal to us. A woman is still missing and possibly deceased. He might be the only link we have if Glynnis Monroe refuses to cooperate. Of course we'll be interviewing all of the members of the Community of Atonement to see what any of them know about Jolene Monroe's disappearance and the possible disappearance of any other members that they know of. This is all just the beginning."

Bree sighed. Yes, it was. None of them knew the breadth or depth of the crimes this cult, and her father, had committed. Murder? Kidnapping? Theft? Assault? The known list was long, so what about the offenses they didn't yet know about? "Yes, sir. You can count on me to find out what I can and report it back to you."

"Thank you, Bree. I know that none of this is easy for you."

"No, sir. It's not."

"You go on home and get some rest. We'll plan to see you tomorrow."

A deputy helped her carry her bags to her car where it was parked out back behind the sheriff's office, while she carried Tiny, who was napping in her arms.

The fifteen-minute drive home seemed to take forever, and by the time she reached her sweet little lake cabin, her eyes were drooping. After Tiny did his business in the grass, the two of them went inside and collapsed on her sofa, snuggled together. Bree fell instantly asleep until she heard someone knocking on the door.

It took Bree a minute to remember where she was and even if it was day or night. The living room was almost dark, so it must be late. She heard the knock again. *Darla.* "I'm coming."

She opened the door and fell into her sister's arms. "I'm so glad you're here." The familiar scent of her lifelong best friend comforted her like nothing else could have in that moment.

Darla pulled her back and looked at her. "What on earth did you do with my sister and why is your hair bright red?"

Bree sniffed and laughed a little despite herself. "Do you like it?"

"You'd be beautiful if you shaved it off. And yes, it's sassy. So, what happened?"

"Daddy's alive. I saw him today."

"Mitch told me."

"He told you? What did he tell you?"

They walked into the living room and sat down together on the sofa, where Tiny had moved to his pillow to continue snoozing. "He said you went undercover and found our father leading a cult."

SUSAN SANDS

Bree nodded. "Yes. Do you remember that awful woman who threw Momma in the dark room to get her sober at the church when we were little? I didn't remember her name from back then, but she had one blue eye and one brown. Her name was Glynnis, and she and Daddy have been going around together to different places over the years and scamming people from what I understand."

"That's horrible. I don't remember her, but I'm not surprised that you do."

"I don't how much of it was her and how much of it was him. She seemed to be in charge, but I can't be sure. He was definitely involved with all of it though. I guess I want to think he's not such a bad person."

"He left us to fend for ourselves with an abusive alcoholic mother. He's a bad person, Bree. He's selfish and has no moral compass, clearly." Darla didn't allow Bree to romanticize their father like she often tried to do. Mainly because she hardly remembered him and had no real affection for him like Bree had. "I'm sorry, sweetie, but he's a piece of shit."

"I know he is. But when I saw him it was like I was ten years old all over again." Bree felt fresh tears threaten. "It was such a shock, Darla."

"I can only imagine. The good news is that he isn't dead, right?" Darla tried to sound positive, Bree could tell.

"That's not even funny. I'm not sure if that would've been better or worse to learn. I just don't know how to feel. The GBI wants me to get information from him about what he's done for their case."

"They want you to rat out your father?"

Bree nodded. "Honestly, it's the right thing to do. I'm

pretty sure he's been party to some pretty awful things."

"Where is he now?"

"He's in the lockup at the sheriff's office in town. We are supposed to go there tomorrow. I have to do an interview with the GBI about our undercover operation. They lost communication while it all went down and I need to fill them in on things that happened just before the team got there."

"I can't believe you did that. I'm impressed, Bree." Bree could see the pride in her sister's gaze.

"I was pretty scared the whole time, so I don't know if it counts."

"It counts. You've always had that kind of courage when it came down to it."

"It helped that I had a team of agents listening to and watching everything we said and did. I never felt alone. And then there was Mitch. He made me feel safe."

"Sounds like he made you feel some other things too." Darla raised her brows suggestively.

"Oh, stop. It wasn't like that. Well, not exactly. He's different than anybody I've ever met." As Bree said it, she was picturing Mitch in her mind and missing him.

"Different how?"

"He's autistic—a little bit. He isn't big on sweet words and manners, but he knows what to say when it matters."

"Like, he's on the spectrum for real?"

Bree nodded. "Yes. I thought he was kind of rude at first when I met him because he was brisk and sort of blew me off. But once he realized he might've offended me, he invited me to have dessert with him and apologized. It was awkward and hard for him but he explained that he's on the autism spectrum and struggles with social situations."

"Does it interfere with his job?" Darla appeared fascinated.

"Well, he's a guy, so being a little less talkative and to the point works around the other special agents. He's a very fact-oriented person and doesn't miss much, so it makes him a fantastic investigator. I guess they deal with some of his small quirks because he's so good at his job."

"That makes sense. He sounded concerned about you when he called."

"I feel like there's a bond between us. Of some sort. I'm not quite sure where we stand personally. He isn't local, so that's not helpful if we were going to try to date."

"Stranger things have happened. It all depends on how much the two of you care about each other and want to be together, I guess. I wouldn't know since I'm single."

"Oh, there's something else."

"What?"

"Daddy mentioned that we have sisters. I don't know how many, but I do know that one of them had died and they found her body. We think Glynnis had something to do with it."

Darla stared at Bree. "You're just now telling me this? Oh, my gosh, Bree. Sisters?"

"It's just all been so much to process today."

"No wonder Mitch was worried about you. So, Daddy not only left us at the mercy of Momma, but he went off and had more daughters with another woman?"

"Women. I think. I didn't get the feeling he got married

and settled with any one woman."

"I guess when you're the big daddy cult guru you get plenty of free lovin' from the groupies. Geez. Can't wait to see what kind of mess he's made of those poor girls. And one died? That's really sad."

"Yes. It's one of the things they're investigating. That's how I got involved in all of this in the first place. They thought the body they found was the wife of Glynnis's son, but turns out it was our sister."

"What a mess. I'm glad you had Mitch call me. I hate that you had to hear all of this on your own." Darla put an arm around Bree.

"You really should consider moving here. We could be spinsters together at least. That might be fun."

Darla sighed. "It's been hard not having you nearby. I've got to tell you that I'm not ruling out the idea. I've got friends and I date a little here and there, but this is a cute town and I could work from home when I'm not traveling."

"So, you'd actually consider moving here with me?" Bree couldn't believe it. Having her sister with her would make her so happy.

"I'll think about it. But I would need my own place. I can't just come here and move in."

"Oh, my gosh. You totally could. We spent our entire childhoods sleeping in the same bedroom—most of the time in the same bed." Bree's memories growing up were filled with Darla's presence even though some of it was dark and scary with Momma. They always had each other's back though.

"Yes, but we aren't kids anymore and I want you to find

someone and make a life with them. I wouldn't want my coming here to keep you from doing that."

"Same here. I want you to find someone and be happy too. Nothing is stopping us from both finding happiness and creating our own families. But it sure would be nice to do it in the same town."

"You're right. It would." Darla laid her head on Bree's shoulder. "I'm so glad I'm here. It's been too long since we've been together."

"It's gonna feel like old times tomorrow because we get to face our past in the form of Daddy after all these years."

"Just so you know, I approve of you finding out every terrible secret he has and telling them all to the GBI or whomever needs them to make all the charges stick. Don't feel guilty about that. You can talk to him and you can even be kind to him, but there are consequences for a life lived in such a selfish and egotistic way—especially since he hurt others."

"Yes, I do want to know what's in his heart and his mind, but I guess both things can happen at the same time. I can learn those things and assist in helping him pay the price for his crimes. I guess the good news is, he can't walk away from us again. But we can certainly walk away from him should we decide to."

"Consider me walked. I've got zero loyalty to him. If I speak to him or am kind to him, it's for your benefit."

The sisters made canned soup and sandwiches like they did as kids when they got hungry, then put on their pajamas and had a much-needed sleepover. Tomorrow would come soon enough.

Chapter Twenty-Three

MITCH SAT WITH Jimmy Lee until almost midnight. He was antsy and worried, but quite relieved to learn that the body they'd found wasn't his precious Jolene.

"Did you know that your momma had a beef with Sarah, Jimmy Lee?" Mitch asked.

Jimmy Lee sighed. "At first she loved her and wanted me to leave Jolene and be with her. I did what she said after Jolene left the compound to keep Momma happy. But Sarah started making noise about Momma being too bossy and trying to keep her from doing what she wanted with the community."

"Like what?"

"She wanted to make it a real nature retreat and only charge the members who joined enough to pay their way and run things. But Momma wanted to make sure nobody left so that she could keep taking their money."

"But Ed wanted to let Sarah try her way of doing things?"

Jimmy Lee nodded. "The master loved Sarah, and Momma got jealous that he was listening to her ideas. They got in a big fight one day and the next day Sarah left. Or that's what Momma told everyone. I guess there was more to it than that."

"Why do you think she ended up with Jolene's clothes and purse on her body?" Mitch was stumped by that.

"I don't know, honestly. Jolene didn't like Sarah because she was sweet on me and Momma liked her. Maybe she helped Momma?"

"Hmm. But what happened to Jolene after that? Do you remember if you heard from Jolene after Sarah left the community?"

"I did. A couple of times. She left the letter, and then another one I didn't tell y'all about, like a week later."

"Why didn't you tell us about it, Jimmy Lee?"

He shrugged. "Wasn't none of anybody's business, I guess."

Mitch didn't understand Jimmy Lee's logic. "Can you show it to me?"

"I burned it. She said she wasn't coming back." He hung his head.

"That would have been something to tell us."

"I kept thinking she would change her mind, you know?"

Mitch thought about that for a minute. "Did Sarah and Jolene look anything alike?"

Jimmy Lee nodded. "Yeah. They did resemble except Sarah had kinda reddish-brown hair. 'Bout the same size too."

Mitch suddenly had a thought. "I'll be right back, Jimmy Lee."

He left the room and did a search for Sarah Hawthorne through his secure GBI server. She appeared to be alive and well and living under the name Sarah Davis with her husband, Calvin Davis in Chattanooga, Tennessee, which was just over the state line from North Georgia. There was a driver's license in the name Sarah Davis that showed a woman that matched the photo of Jolene they'd found in the purse, aside from her having auburn hair. "Well, I'll be."

How was he going to break this to poor Jimmy Lee? What a blow. Mitch would need to bring Jolene/Sarah in for questioning to find out if she had anything to do with Sarah's murder, and to figure out what kind of charges they would pursue against her for impersonating the real Sarah Hawthorne. What a mess.

He cut Jimmy Lee loose without enlightening him regarding this new information about Jolene. No need to ruin his day after everything he'd been through the past couple of weeks—years. Once they'd spoken with Jolene, Mitch would bring him back in and maybe he would convince Jolene to meet with him face-to-face as she should.

This case was going to age Mitch. There weren't any happy endings sometimes. In this instance, finding the killer meant opening up a whole slew of other investigations. Glynnis wasn't only guilty of murder, she was also guilty of child abuse, battery, theft, kidnapping, gun charges, and who knew what else. And Ed Hawthorne, a.k.a. the master— they'd be trying to figure out his role in all of this for months. Plus, in the coming weeks, they'd be questioning every person they could find who had ever been associated with the Community of Atonement to help gather evidence and find all of the guilty parties.

Parsing through the statements and comparing facts was

a painstaking process to ready it all for a prosecution team. It would take months, maybe more than a year. He hadn't yet spoken to Ed Hawthorne, Bree's dad. Mitch really hoped she was handling all of this okay with the help of her sister. Thing had gotten muddy now that she was personally involved with the suspects and the victim. Not to mention her role with the investigation.

Mitch had a very strong code when it came to mixing work with his personal life, and he'd nearly crossed that line with Bree. His emotions had become involved. Now, with the rest of it getting so messy, he couldn't see things clearly unless he broke away from her and stayed focused on the investigation. Yes, he liked her—maybe he'd even been falling in love with her. But the way his brain worked, he couldn't do both at the same time. Work and love. Not like this.

He would need to speak with her at some point and it was something he dreaded.

BREE AND DARLA got dressed the next morning and headed over to the sheriff's office in town. Bree was nervous about seeing Daddy, and she was nervous about seeing Mitch again. He'd pretty much handed her off to Darla and gone back to work, which made sense since he had a lot to do to get to the bottom of everything that had happened. But still, she'd been thinking about him despite everything that had gone down and she wondered if he'd spared her a thought.

She knew that he compartmentalized things because

she'd watched him work. He was efficient because he could block out his emotions. But did that mean he could block them out indefinitely?

Hannah waved Bree over when they arrived. "Special Agent Roberts wants to see you. Said to tell you to find him as soon as you got here."

"Okay. Hannah, this is my sister, Darla."

"Nice to meet you." The two women exchanged pleasantries. "Darla, you can wait out here if you want while Bree meets with the special agent."

"Thanks."

"Follow me and I'll introduce you to everyone first, and then you can come back here," Bree suggested.

Bree led Darla to the conference room. As they made their way back, several of the officers and special agents said hello and told Bree, "Nice job."

When they entered the conference room, Bree noticed that Mitch was there with Aaron Roberts. The two looked to be in a deep discussion, and only looked up when they heard the door click shut behind Bree and Darla. Mitch looked up and his eyes locked with Bree's.

"Oh, hi." He didn't smile, but his gaze never wavered from hers.

"This is my sister, Darla. Darla, this is Mitch Calloway and Special Agent Roberts."

"Nice to meet you." Darla nodded to each and smiled.

Aaron Roberts appeared to be caught unaware when he saw Darla. He cleared his throat. "Oh, hi. Nice to meet you." He stood and put out his hand.

Darla shook it. The two exchanged a glance and their

handshake held an extra second before Darla pulled her hand away gently.

"You wanted to see me?" Bree asked Aaron Roberts, breaking the odd connection between the two.

"Oh, yes, Bree. You and I need to sit down and go through the events that occurred yesterday before the team came in. Mitch will sit in if that's all right."

"Of course."

"I'll just be in the waiting area with Hannah." Darla pointed toward the door. "See you in a bit." She smiled. "Nice meeting you both."

Again, Bree noted how oddly Roberts stared after Darla as she exited the room. Like he was instantly smitten. So interesting.

"Have a seat, Bree." Mitch stood and pulled out a chair for her. His expression was guarded.

"Thanks."

"Can you give us a recounting of what happened from the time you were taken to the office on the compound? What was said and by whom, anything of note. What you saw and heard starting from the beginning until the agents came through the door."

Bree began the retelling. She described what she'd seen, heard, and how she'd felt. When it came to seeing Daddy, it got a little harder. Especially when he discussed leaving the family for a better life. And having more children. Then, when Glynnis came in with the gun, and how they both knew she was lying about Sarah. By the time she'd finished, she had tears tracking down her cheeks.

She'd seen Mitch stiffen several times as she described

the scene. Bree knew he wasn't all business here, and that her emotions affected him. At least there was that.

"I'm so sorry you had to endure that kind of trauma, Bree. Of course, none of us had any idea that your father was part of this investigation. What a bizarre coincidence." Aaron Roberts lent her some empathy as well. "If you think of any other details, please give us a call."

"Of course. I'd like to see my daddy if that's all right. Is there anything specifically you want me to ask him?" Bree asked.

"We haven't yet interviewed him, so there's a lot to unpack. He's requested an attorney, and we're waiting until his counsel arrives to speak with him. I can't ask you to collect information from him in an official capacity, but learn what you can, and if you feel compelled, we'd like to know what you learn. Obviously, you can visit him in lockup until he's arraigned. We've got to figure out what to charge him with first."

"I'll see what he has to say." Bree stood.

Mitch stood as well. "Today will be spent speaking with witnesses and interviewing Glynnis. Her attorney is already on the way, so we're hoping she'll give us some information about Ed Hawthorne and then he can tell us more about her role in all of this when we are able to interview him."

"I know you won't be able to share everything about the case with me since he's my father, but I'll tell you if I learn anything new on this end. I would like to know if you find out about Jolene. I'm really curious to know what happened to her."

"The only thing I can share right now is that we believe

she's alive and using Sarah Hawthorne's identity. We don't know if she was involved in Sarah's murder. Obviously, that's another situation that's going to take some further investigation. Of course, I'll ask that you don't share that with anyone since it's still an ongoing case. We haven't informed Jimmy Lee yet."

"Wow. I'm glad she's alive. That's a real kick in the teeth for Jimmy Lee, poor guy. Tell him if he needs to talk to someone, he knows where to find me." Bree felt awful knowing that Jolene had taken off after everything Jimmy Lee had done to make a life for the two of them. No wonder she hadn't come back for Tiny. It would've tipped everyone off.

Bree looked over at Mitch, who was making notes and *not* making eye contact with her. "Well, I guess I'll head to the lockup with Darla to see Daddy. I'll see you both later."

"Do you want me to go with you?" Mitch asked, still avoiding her gaze.

Bree shook her head sadly. She could tell that he'd distanced himself from her as he worked to solve the case. "No, Darla is with me."

Mitch looked up at her then. "Take care, Bree."

So, that was it. *Take care, Bree.* "You too, Mitch."

Bree and Darla made their way to the lockup where their father waited, and Bree couldn't help but feel completely bereft by Mitch's dismissal of her. She'd believed that after all of this was over that maybe there would be something left between them.

Hadn't he said he hoped to see her again? Despite not wanting to fall for him, she'd gone and foolishly done so.

He'd made it clear that he couldn't or wouldn't allow his feelings for her to get in the way of his job. And there was no way she was going to humiliate herself for a man's affection ever again—even Mitch. Even if it broke her heart—again.

MITCH WAS SITTING at a table in Chelsey's Bar, not far from the office, surrounded by his peers, mostly guys from the office where he worked. They were celebrating solving the case, and the guys were raising a glass to him. He had to admit that it felt good to be toasted and admired for his hard work. He'd spent a lot of time and effort getting to this moment in his career—and his life.

"Here's to Mitch—the guy who never gives up and always finds a way to solve the hard cases." Aaron Roberts, his boss, made the toast.

"Hear, hear," the group all murmured enthusiastically.

They'd enjoyed a dinner of pub food and a few beers, knowing they had deputies at the ready to drive them home on this particular evening.

As Mitch stood and shook several of the other special agents' hands, he noticed a man out of the corner of his eye sitting at the bar. Watching. His father. He barely recognized him because he'd gotten old since the last time they'd actually spoken face-to-face.

As the others made their way outside, Mitch paused a second, deciding if he should waste his time and breath speaking to the man who'd so deeply disappointed him growing up. Before he'd decided, his dad motioned for

Mitch to come over. *Damn.* He couldn't avoid it now.

Mitch made his way to the bar. "Hi, Dad."

"Looks like you've done yourself proud there." He motioned toward Mitch's badge clipped to his belt. "I noticed your fellow officers toasting you. You must've done something really great, son."

Mitch saw something cross his father's weathered face that looked like pride. "Yeah. I did. I solved a big case and saved a few lives. It happens now and then. Pretty good for a sad little loser, huh?" Mitch repeated something his father had said to him once after he'd struck out during a baseball game as a freshman in high school.

"Oh, son, you know I didn't mean that. I was just trying to motivate you—get you to try harder."

Mitch shook his head. "I'm doing great, Dad, despite you. Mom's doing great too. Looks like I didn't need motivating." And in that moment, Mitch realized it was true. He didn't need his father's approval to feel successful, and he certainly wasn't going to turn out like him—a man who was an emotional desert, unable to commit and stay committed to those he cared about. His worth as a man wasn't tied to his father in any way but he hadn't realized that until now. "See you around, Dad."

Chapter Twenty-Four

Six Months Later

BREE AND DARLA were on their way to the annual
Moonshine Christmas Tree Lighting. Darla was meeting Special Agent Aaron Roberts there. They'd been seeing
each other casually since they'd met in June. Aaron had it
pretty bad for Darla, but she was taking it slower. Bree knew
that secretly Darla was crazy about the upstanding lawman,
but terrified of getting her heart broken. Darla had moved to
Moonshine and in with Bree not long after they'd found
Daddy.

Bree parked in her dedicated parking space in front of
her office near the town square. It was a great perk during
the Christmas season when parking was at a premium. The
two women were bundled up in coats and scarves and each
carrying a box of ornaments to hang on the tree. Both were
looking forward to meeting up with now-mutual friends
Sadie, Merilee, and Jennifer. Their three younger half sisters
and Tess, Sarah's mom, were all meeting them a little later.
They found their small group near the hot cocoa stand by
the ice cream shop. "Hi there. I can't believe how cold it is
tonight." Bree hugged Jennifer's neck and then the others.

"There you are." A deep voice sounded just behind them.

It was Aaron speaking to Darla. She lit up at the sound of his voice.

"Hi, Bree." She froze at hearing the second male voice. She would've recognized it anywhere. Turning, she looked into the gorgeous eyes of Mitch Calloway.

"Hi, Mitch. I didn't expect to see you tonight." Understatement.

"Aaron suggested I accompany him. I hope you don't mind." He grinned at her, causing her heart to double time. It also brought back the crushing disappointment she'd felt when she'd left the sheriff's office six months ago after he'd casually dismissed her.

Instead of telling him that, she said, "It's nice to see you. How's the case going?" They hadn't spoken since the GBI had moved the investigation back to their offices and out of Moonshine. Bree's feelings had been hurt—more than hurt—but after spending a lot of time thinking about it, she'd decided that maybe it was for the best since she understood that Mitch wasn't cut out for long-term emotional attachment. Or that's what she'd told herself.

"We're going to trial soon. I guess you've spoken to your father about it."

"Not much. We aren't really in contact except to discuss the whereabouts of my sisters." Bree and Darla had made peace with Daddy while he'd been incarcerated but had decided that he wasn't someone they needed in their lives. They did, however, insist that he tell them everything he knew about their three half sisters. Their ages ranged between eighteen and twenty-four. The girls thought it was great fun to have motherly older sisters, and they all met up every month for dinner. Fortunately, they all lived in a fifty-mile radius.

They'd had a celebration of life for Sarah, and met her mother, Tess, an aging hippie, who'd been estranged from her, but who'd surprisingly bonded with Bree and Darla and the other girls. They now included Tess in their monthly dinners. It was an odd group of women who now felt like family. The others should be along anytime now for the tree-lighting ceremony.

So, Bree had settled in and found her place and her family in Moonshine without requiring a man to complete her picture. And yet, as she looked into Mitch's familiar gaze, she couldn't help wondering what that might've been like.

Mitch gently took her hand and led her away from the group so that they could speak without yelling. "So, Bree. I was wondering if you'd like to go out to dinner sometime soon?"

"Like on a date?" she asked, noticing the warm glimmer in his gaze.

"Like on a lot of dates." Mitch grinned at her. "If it's not too late."

"But why now?"

"I'm so sorry for not calling you sooner. I haven't stopped thinking about you since we met. But I didn't want to lead you into a relationship that I couldn't maintain. I mean, I wasn't sure if I could do it. Because of my deficiencies, you know? I ran into my dad a while back and I realized that I'm nothing like him and never will be. I'll still be me, and well, that's always a bit of a struggle, but I know that I'm ready—that I can be with you. I'm back in therapy, and I believe that you get me like nobody ever has. Would you be willing to give me a chance?"

"You went to therapy for me?" she asked.

"For us. So, what do you say?"

"I'd be more than willing." He gathered her in his arms and kissed her like she'd been wishing he would since the moment they'd met.

Epilogue

THE JUDGE'S GAVEL made Bree jump. "Case adjourned."

"Well I guess that's that then, huh?" Darla looked over at Bree. "I'm glad it's finally over."

"Me too." The two-month trial had been enlightening and exhausting. Daddy was found guilty of several crimes. Accessory to commit them mostly. Glynnis had turned out to be the main perpetrator of the evil against the people she'd come in contact with. Negligent homicide included. Daddy hadn't had any part in that, thankfully.

Glynnis had pushed Sarah and she'd hit her head on the corner of a table and that had killed her. Then, she'd covered it up. Apparently, Jolene had witnessed Glynnis dragging Sarah's body and followed her to the gravel pit. After Glynnis left, Jolene was the one who'd dressed Sarah's body in her own clothes and placed the identifying items to fake her death in case Sarah's remains were ever found. Glynnis hadn't known about it. Jolene wanted out. Out of her marriage with Jimmy Lee and his mental health problems, out of the cult and away from Glynnis, and out of her own life.

Jolene just happened on the opportunity of Glynnis burying Sarah. Jimmy Lee was the victim of Glynnis and of

Jolene. Both women had wronged him and Bree hoped that someday he would heal emotionally. Right now, she was counseling him to continue with his meds and helping him bolster his self-esteem after such emotional trauma. Fortunately, he wasn't an especially deep thinker, so that helped.

The other victims of Glynnis and Daddy were the members of the Community of Atonement. Most were welcomed back by their families with open arms, but they'd had a number done on them financially and mentally, so the money from all of the community's bank accounts, along with the sale of the compound and the land, had been dispersed to help cover their losses. There would be lawsuits on top of lawsuits but Glynnis was never getting out of prison, and when or if Daddy ever did, he wouldn't have a dime to his name.

Darla and Aaron became engaged a month before Bree and Mitch, and as cheesy as a double wedding might sound, the two sisters decided it was perfect for the two of them. There was the matter of both Aaron and Mitch not living in the same town as their brides-to-be, but that was being worked out. Since the GBI had field offices all over the state, transfers were applied for, and one way or another, they would all live nearby. The half-sisters would be bridesmaids, along with Sadie, Jennifer, and Merilee. Tess, Sarah's mom, would stand in as mother of the brides. Chase and Randy would walk the brides down the aisle.

Tiny, who'd proudly gotten used to walking more instead of being carried around in Bree's purse, would be the ring bearer—of course.

The End

I hope you enjoyed WHAT THEY DON'T KNOW! Get ready for the next installment in the Moonshine, Georgia series releasing in 2026!

Here's a sneak peek:

Artist Randi Collins was presumed dead at sixteen when she'd run away from home as a massive category five hurricane hit her hometown near coastal Galliano, Louisiana. Dani had been quite literally swept away and lost in the storm, injured, and displaced for months afterward. When she finally returned, her home and her mother were, quite literally, gone without a trace.

Now, Randi, who's changed her name to Randi Jessamine, is living and working at an artist colony when a handsome federal agent with a badge shows up at her door looking for a missing woman named Randi Collins.

Randi has her reasons for not wanting to be found, and Agent Jeff Price has a job to do. Randi learns that her mother gave her identity to another young woman after the hurricane, and now the two must meet to resolve the questions both women still have regarding their pasts.

Jeff Price is as stubborn as he is attractive, and Randi has a hard time ignoring him during their trip to Moonshine, Georgia, together no matter how hard she tries. Can they fight the attraction between? Should they?

Dear Reader,

What They Don't Know is my very first "Whodunnit." I feel like I've been moving in the direction of a murder mystery for a long time, and the added cult element set in the North Georgia Mountains seemed the perfect place to find buried bones at the bottom of a gravel pit.

It was such fun to write and I hope you enjoy following Bree and Mitch on their twisting quest to uncover layers of truths neither could have imagined.

With every story I write, there are people who help me pretend I know exactly what and how things work in my made-up world. Sending huge thanks to my neighbor Megan Pettis, former NOPD police office turned attorney, and friend to my puppy, Petunia. Megan's patient explanations about how things work within the law enforcement community were invaluable in helping me write accurate investigative and procedural scenes.

As always I thank my writing tribe both local and online for their constant support. Thanks to the amazing Tule team and my editor, Sinclair Sawhney, who always make my books better. Thank you to Doug, my husband, who rarely hears my thanks out loud but bears the brunt of my deadlines and no dinner without complaint. To my mom, Linda Noel, who reads everything I write and tells me how awesome I am—always.

All the best!
Susan Sands

If you enjoyed *What They Don't Know*,
you'll love the other books in the…

Moonshine series
Book 1: *Her Missing Pieces*
Book 2: *A Georgia Christmas*
Book 3: *What They Don't Know*

Available now at your favorite online retailer!

More Books by Susan Sands

Louisiana series

Book 1: *Home to Cypress Bayou*
Book 2: *Secrets in Cypress Bayou*
Book 3: *A Bayou Christmas*
Book 4: *Bayou Redemption*

The Alabama series

Book 1: *Again, Alabama*
Book 2: *Love, Alabama*
Book 3: *Forever, Alabama*
Book 4: *Christmas, Alabama*
Book 5: *Noel, Alabama*

Available now at your favorite online retailer!

About the Author

Susan Sands grew up in a real life Southern Footloose town, complete with her senior class hosting the first ever prom in the history of their tiny public school. Is it any wonder she writes Southern small town stories full of porch swings, fun and romance?

Susan lives in suburban Atlanta surrounded by her husband, three young adult kiddos and lots of material for her next book.

Thank you for reading

What They Don't Know

If you enjoyed this book, you can find more from all our great authors at TulePublishing.com, or from your favorite online retailer.

TULE
PUBLISHING